The Crown of the Sea

Also by Sara Salam

If Water Were Fire, A Novel

If Love Were Salt, A Novel

The Mind Is Just Like A Muscle: A Self-Help Book For Teens On Growing Up in Modern America

How to Write a Résumé: Finding a Job in Any Job Market

My Truth Journal

Love Isn't Linear: A Collection of Poems About Modern Love

My Newport: A Collection of Poems About Newport Beach, California

Remember When: A Collection of Poems By A Lovestruck Teen Who Had The Courage to Dream

The Crown of the Sea

By
Sara Salam

The Peacock Pen Press
2021

Copyright © 2021 Sara Salam
All rights reserved. No part of this book may be used in any manner whatsoever without written permission, except in the case of brief quotations and reviews.

ISBN: 978-1-953636-09-6 (Paperback)
ISBN: 978-1-953636-10-2 (eBook)

Library of Congress Control Number: 2021910450

1. Contemporary Romance.
2. New Adult Romance.
3. Love Stories.
4. Contemporary Women's Fiction.
5. Women's Literature & Fiction.
6. Fan Fiction.

This is a work of fiction. Names, characters, places, and incidents are either the product of the author's imagination or are used fictitiously, and any resemblance to actual persons, living or dead, businesses, companies, events, or locales is entirely coincidental.

Book cover design by Aspen Denita.
Author portrait by Christina Wehbe.

Icons from The Noun Project: sun by Ralf Schmitzer; helm by Rusty Copperpot; sailboat by Rusty Copperpot; anchor by Rusty Copperpot; lighthouse by Rusty Copperpot; wave by Rusty Copperpot.

Printed by The Peacock Pen Press in the United States of America.

First Printing Edition 2021.

To join Sara Salam's email list for updates on her books, scan the QR code below:

© 2021 Sara Salam

🌐 www.bysarasalam.com

📷 @bysarasalam

▶ Sara Salam

With inspiration from AHF, my mirror.

Contents

Part One: The Courtship   1

Part Two: The Marriage   133

"I can't control how you feel about me, any more than I can control when the sun rises, or that it rises at all."

Part One:
The Courtship

Chapter 1
Diana
2019

"She's my one true love."

That did it.

That hurt; it's palpable now. Before, it was dormant, a bear hibernating during a white, English winter.

Now? It sears. A wound ripped open, where scabs once protected the inside from the outside. Tenuous and temporary, scabs inevitably fall off.

I'm falling now. Floating, even. My heart doesn't carry the weight of an anchor, cast overboard to slow and ultimately stop forward progress. Maybe to Charles I am an anchor, weighed down at port. And Camilla is his compass, his headwind, wrapped into the meager body of a wannabe trophy wife who wasn't quite the trophy his family had in mind.

Me, I was the trophy—the chosen one, the one who came from (enough) money. The girl whose athletic build and perky breasts made her the envy of every cheerleader and wet dream of every football player at Eastcliff High. The girl who wanted for nothing, yet already had everything.

Everything except a life of her own.

He lied to me, I could say. But I'm not vindictive.

She stole him from me, I could sob. But I'm not sad.

They deceived me, I could blame. But I'm not ashamed.

Charles and Camilla have loved since love was a love song, named for Solomon. He and his quiet manners; she and her finesse with boats.

"She soothes me even when I don't think I need it," he tells me. "How do you give that up—someone who knows you better than you know yourself?"

I wouldn't know what that feels like, I think, *because I know me better than anyone knows me.*

I'm a mess, plain and simple. In love, and in loss.

The sky falls in pieces. It changes color first, and before you know it, night arrives and there's no light but for the balls of fire burning millions of miles away. So far away.

Newport, my home with its lights that speckle the bay, moves and shakes me like a quake all too familiar to this tectonic plate. A bedazzled paradise easily hides what is both a haven and a haunting.

"She has good sense," Elizabeth, his Mum, would say of me. "She'll love you and support you. She won't get in your way."

I got in my own way.

The ferries cross the harbor back and forth, intercepting sea lions. Cormorants hang their wings to dry like open books. Paddle boarders navigate dinghies and docks to avoid being crunched in the wake of *Invictus*. The water looks of satin bed sheets after a night of not sleeping.

I don't sleep anymore; I dream. I dream of a revisionist life, one where I noticed the signs and ceased losing myself so he could find himself.

So he could find himself in her.

In her . . .

"I thought we were it, the end game." I was a truth-teller.

"I never loved you." He was a liar.

"Whatever love means."

Chapter 2
Charles
2019

There's nothing worse than betrayal. How could she do this? One minute we're sitting here, living our married life over eggs Benedict and our respective versions of good coffee. Mine is simple: black. Hers is some version of a Starbucks concoction that I can't pronounce. It's not the happiest, but it's real. Then, the next minute, our lives blow up in smoke like a burning pile of manure—putrid and suffocating.

"She's my one true love." I didn't know what else to say but the truth. We've been through hell and high water, so isn't it time for honesty?

"I thought we were it, the endgame. I tried so hard to be what you need, but it never worked. I loved you so much. It wasn't enough."

Diana's hysterics echo through the otherwise quiet nook. The remnants of our time together are scattered around us: the red orchids I bought her, the spoon rest she bought me (though I'm not sure why, I don't cook). Kitchens are where big things happen, apparently. Kitchens and bathrooms.

I get up from behind the table, a two-seater perfect for a couple, and then I pace, shaking my hands like they're wet with water. I want to throw something, but I know better. The staff would hear and call the police. I don't need that kind of trouble right now. I need a drink.

Yes, a drink. Whiskey, maybe. It's before noon, but hey, desperate times.

As I pour my Blue Label over an ice ball, I hear white noise that can only be coming from Diana. I focus on the glass in front of me until, finally, there is silence.

"I never loved you."

I'm spiteful and angry, livid, at this woman—*my wife*—for taking such deceptive actions. She gets me so nuts sometimes, I say things I don't mean.

I loved her, once upon a time. And I still love her, as someone would love the mother of their children. I just don't love her in the way she wants to be loved.

Chapter 3
Camilla
1998

"Ease the jib sheet!"

I trim the sail like a skilled hair stylist wielding her sheers. Charles secures the line like the novice sailor he is. He takes direction well, at least. It's one of his best traits.

Me? I'm more of a rogue wanderer; a rolling tide. Like the currents that carry these sabots across the open sea—unpredictable. All natural. Nothing tethers me, not even the line of a mast.

Except maybe him.

We're not a "smart match," as they might say among British royalty.

We're also an unlikely friendship.

He, with his silences interspersed with pockets of power trips and panic attacks.

Me, with my brazen heart and emotive minefields.

It didn't start out that way.

It starts at a dinner party celebrating Titi's thirtieth birthday at the Balboa Bay Club. My name card rests inconspicuously atop the off-white linen, positioned slightly above the floating anchor centered in the china pattern. His name card is to the right of mine:

Charles Windsor.

"Do you enjoy sea bass? They have the best sea bass chili." Charles sets down his tumbler of what looks like an old fashioned while taking his seat next to me.

What the F is sea bass chili? That can't possibly be a thing, a fish-based chili. Stew? Definitely. Chili? Not so much.

"I don't enjoy such things, but I'm sure you'll let me know how it tastes."

He seems amused by my response. I know this because he says, "I'm amused by your response." I'll learn Charles leaves nothing to the imagination, including secret encounters at the Emerald Bay estate that are cloaked in shame and serenades.

"You're amused? Or bemused?" Wordplay tickles my mind like a feather to a child's nose.

"What's the difference?"

"If you have to ask—"

Copper mule mugs clang throughout the dining hall. Titi's husband, Paul, bestows a silence among the crowd as only a nine-figure financier can. Cameras manned by the token few invited paparazzi flash choicely at only the most photographable moments; it is a condition of their access to this event.

Charles and I exchange glances like we're sharing a secret neither of us knows, but are willing to keep. We bond through Balboa's bastion of bad appetizers and even worse music selection.

It sounds like the seventies in here.

"Friends!" Paul's baritone octave booms between the vaulted ceilings and coastal glam decor that typify the space. Onlookers dressed in Chanel and Gucci classics juxtapose themselves with the high-end casual setting, an irony of the Newport story. "Today, we celebrate my love, my wife, Titi the tenacious, the top of the hub, the tigress of ti—"

"Paul!" Titi slaps his arm playfully, tacitly admitting to the accusation that remains a tethered tie, but only between the two of them.

At that moment, Charles taps my elbow. Conspiratorially, he points to the alcove behind the untended bar. No one would see us leave, we're so far removed from the titular characters of the evening.

We sneak away silently without fanfare. He pours me a glass of Veuve Yellow Label.

"Having fun yet?" I ask more questions than I answer. We *cheers* our effortless escape in sync with the birthday toast.

"What if I kissed you right now?" He is bold yet bidding, a regular regalist who doesn't subscribe to any convention but his own.

"I don't worry about what-ifs." I sip my champagne simply. "I'm more interested in what *is*."

Chapter 4
Diana
2007

These days and nights are all the same: bathed in frivolous pastimes and expensive champagne. I like expensive champagne. I'm groomed to enjoy expensive champagne and its partners in crime: caviar, strawberries, and Kobe beef.

I don't pretend to hate it. I've accepted my role in life: the Barbie. The Blond Bombshell. The former Miss America contestant. A USC Song Girl. Proud member of too many golf and yacht clubs. Even if I could control the amount of privilege I was born into, I don't know what I'd choose for myself. This is all I know.

I wouldn't call my childhood happy. It was actually more unhappy and detached. One time, I saw my dad slap my mom across the face while I was hiding behind a door. I have a tendency to hide behind doors, and when I do, I never see anything good. It's a bad habit that leads to nothing but negative experiences. When will I ever learn?

I get tired of being an adult. I don't enjoy attention, the spotlight, being the center attraction of a follow spot on stage at Lincoln Center. I'm not Misty Copeland. Dancing has always made me happy, but that's where our similarities end. My ankles were never strong enough. Being a song girl requires a different sort of skill.

"Your smile is radiant," they'd tell me. "You could light up a room with those eyes."

Ah, beauty. Such an ephemeral concept, at least in the physical sense.

What kind of beauty endures? Some say everything is temporary.

Even love.

"Come! You'll have a good time once you're there, I *promise*."

My sister, Sarah, never passes up an opportunity to celebrate anything, especially the Fourth of July.

The Fourth of July in Newport is like Inauguration Day, where patriotism shows up yet the true purpose of the pomp is the party itself, the people who throw it, and the principles they represent. There are fireworks, lots of them, all viewable within a five-mile radius. The peninsula, where the parity of wealth in this town is most apparent, shuts down all vehicular traffic in an attempt to contain the litany of loud debauchery that riddles the streets. The Fourth falls on a Saturday this year, ensuring a bristling bounty of bros, babes, and beers aplenty.

"I really don't feel like going." I just got back from BVI a few days ago, and I'm still jetlagged. "I really won't be much fun." It's all I can say to show her how my attitude will affect her good time. Classic bail tactic: Always make it about them and how their good time will be compromised. Sometimes it works; sometimes it doesn't.

"But I need you. I can't face Charles alone."

Ah, I get it now. Charles, the long-last ex-boyfriend from many moons ago, who up and ended their tryst because, well, she had it coming.

I love my sister, but when you essentially defame your boyfriend's family and accuse them of illegitimately building their real estate empire, what do you expect?

"You're lucky he didn't sue you." I'm sensitive when I want to be. "He could've ended you." I'm also dramatic when I want to be. (The drama doesn't make it untrue. The power of this family is comparable to that of the British monarchy, minus the crown jewels.) Usually my sister gets the brunt of it. Come hell or high water, she will always be my sister. That shit is permanent.

"See? I need protection! What if one of his bodyguards jumps me and take me into custody? You might never see me again!" Of the two of us, her flare for the dramatic is more fiery than mine.

Mine is more like a candle, where hers is a billowing bonfire that was once the W Tower at the Wedge.

My body's fight response is waning.

"Fine, *fineeeee,* I'll go with you. But I'm only staying for an hour. That should be enough time to gauge Charles' assassination efforts or lack thereof. Cool?"

"Ughhhhhhh, fine. I'm not worried. I bet you'll want to stay anyway."

The party hosts belong to the upper echelons of high Newport Society. I call them the Drone Rangers. The parents are heirs to the highest-grossing drone security company in the world. Their only child, a real estate agent named Taylor, is Charles' best friend. They went to Mater Dei and Stanford together.

Their home borders the Boardwalk, a three-ish-mile stretch of sidewalk that hugs the coastline from 36th Street to E Street. Mediterranean in style, the fact that it's not a modern farmhouse white box is one of its most redeeming qualities. Built in the mid-2000s, it boasts a third-story jacuzzi and deck with all the fixings. The decor is coastal chic with a vintage flair. It's more Restoration Hardware than Tommy Bahama.

Did I mention this is their second home?

Their primary residence is in Newport Coast, gate-guarded and locked away from the wandering eyes of mere mortals. Most images captured by the paparazzi are of the wrought iron spears that separate private from public.

"Any Joe-Blow-Schmo could meander in and out, and we wouldn't know the difference." Mr. Perry is the most rational of the Perry clan. Obviously the threat of an interloper wasn't enough to deter them from buying the property in the first place. I question his motives.

Taylor uses this locale as his crash pad when he's not abroad, courting international clients in Dubai. His parents aren't here much. They split time between Casa Drone and their chalet in Vail, and are about to close on a chateau in France. Apparently Mrs. Perry has recently taken up winemaking as a hobby, behind her affinity for underwater basket-weaving.

"Happy Fourth!" rings redundantly as we approach the house. We enter from the alley side, where there's a carport adjacent to the patio garden. It's a double-lot home. The rich like to stake their claims.

Half-naked women ranging from their twenties into their forties run amuck, their scantily clad bodies emitting glows on the order of natural to orange. Pasties in the shape of stars and streamers abound, adhered to cover only the most private of lady parts. Compared to this lot, Sarah and I look like nuns in our cutoffs and tank tops.

"Oh God, he's right there."

We're not twenty steps into the soiree when Charles appears from behind the bar, backlit by abalone and other exotic shellfish. Sarah tosses her hair in an attempt to sexify her otherwise conservative look.

"If I dress more casual, my new hair will be more noticeable," she had commented as we were getting ready. She just got highlights and a rather bold asymmetrical cut. She pulls it off well. Leave it to her to be ready with a strategy to show it off.

I fall back into my role of spectator and prepare to watch the engagement unfold.

Only, it doesn't go as I would've expected.

"Sarah, hun, how are you? Long time. Glad you could make it." Charles appears to be mostly sober, maybe a tad buzzed by the Veuve that occupies his right hand, but he's by all accounts cordial and, dare I say, dignified. Must be the Topsiders and Nantucket reds. He belongs in a Vineyard Vines ad.

Not one to pass up an opportunity for a compliment, Sarah responds, "You know I always love a good party. Tay's family are always such gracious hosts. Plus, it's the perfect place to show off my new 'do." She tucks a few loose strands behind her ear and flashes him the Spencer smile. It runs in the family, not like her bold antics. Those are hers alone.

"Ah, yes, very nice." Still cordial and dignified, if not predictable.

As soon as "nice" leaves his lips, a moment of magic unfolds. As soon as Sarah is called away by a college friend. As soon as Charles pierces my soul with those eyes. As soon as he makes me the best champagne offer of my life. As soon as we're somehow left alone.

As soon as fireworks fly.

Chapter 5
Charles
2007

She reminds me of someone. Someone I know intimately well. Someone whose shoes I've walked, run, and swum in for miles along the coast. (Though I'm largely unathletic and clumsy. Just ask Camilla.) A kindred.

She reminds me of myself.

When I take her hand and pull her towards the hay bale that is the running joke of the Perry family (a tribute to their Western heritage, no less), there's nothing but peace. At least, I think it's peace. It doesn't have the narking barking I'm so used to, the agony that tends to reverberate in the hollows of my conscious mind. I know they're not hollow, but it feels that way, like an evaporated pool of saltwater where nothing remains but the sodium crystals. It's a struggle to stay hopeful, to keep fear at bay. When fear comes to play, my cave is my sanctuary.

There's not much to it, only that it's mine and mine alone. I don't have that in other aspects of my life. My home is a gilded cage and I am the voiceless songbird trapped within it. It is a quilted, cool chaos that blankets every aspect of my life, including my upending search for love. A search which, if I had my way, I would maybe table forever. I don't love. I don't believe myself capable of loving. I have a tendency to date unavailable women for this reason. It makes me feel safe, protected. As if I live in a bulletproof glass house: I can witness the world from inside, but am hidden from the wind, rain, and women on the prowl.

"You looked so sad," she says to me after we trade life updates and other such expected pleasantries. She speaks of my expression while I looked on towards the casket that bedded my dead uncle during his burial mass at the chapel down the street. I didn't realize she attended. I didn't see her there. But then, how does one see through a wall of tears?

"I am sad." It's the truth. Probably more than she can realize in this moment. Maybe more than she can realize, ever. I've never met anyone so capable, except maybe Camilla. Camilla doesn't enable me, though. She supports me. She listens to me. I've never had her sympathy.

Diana takes my hand in hers. Amidst the drunken revelers that raid liquor storage and wine cabinets, we share a moment. Perhaps we share something more than that. We share understanding. We're cut from the same cloth, she and I. Her dad is a financial adviser for my family's firm. They golf and shoot the shit at least once a week at the club. He's not an employee, though, which honestly makes it better. We're more equal that way.

And she's hot. I enjoy looking at her, with her platinum blonde hair and perfectly proportioned figure. To touch her all night? What a fantasy. Isn't that what love means, to have and to hold?

"You should be with someone who will look after you." Diana will love, cherish, and obey me, when given the chance. Why?

Because she pities me. This beautiful, young (sub-thirty), smokeshow. My future wife.

I think I'm okay with that.

Chapter 6
Camilla
1998

"Ask me a question."

I've learned Charles, when left to his own devices, is a bit of a chatterbox. Chatterbox Chuck. He just needs to be nudged a bit.

"What's your favorite color?" Not what I expected, but at least he takes direction well.

"It changes, like a mood ring." I didn't realize this was an answer until posed with the question. Funny how that works. "But on any given day, I'd say a turquoise-y blue. Like shallow waters in Hawaii. How about you?"

"Mine is blue, too."

"What kind of blue?"

"A dark blue."

"Navy? Cobalt? Sapphire?"

"How do you know so much about colors?"

Finally, a question without being prompted.

We're puttering along the docks at the Lido Marina, passing the nautical-themed food establishments on the left and the mooring-sprinkled harbor on the right. Sometimes I feel like a tourist in my town, but I don't mind it. Not when the view looks like this and my companion looks like that.

It's more than his looks, though. I didn't even find him attractive when we first met at that dinner party. Conventionally attractive, yes. He has the face of a cologne model: an angular chin accented by eyes with the longest lashes I've ever seen. Not really my type. My type is more Andrew, the beachy, blonde, surfer-turned-sophisticate. It's that sometimes, Charles' charm catches me off guard and I forget to breathe.

"I don't know, I guess it's the creative side of me. I like making different color combinations, especially with clothes and decorating." I pause; do I share more? "I redo my interior decor every few years just because I think it's fun to try out new designs and combine motifs that may not at first look like they go together, but somehow do. It's like a treasure hunt, but for a vibe, not a diamond."

"I can see that. You dress well." One of his few spoken compliments.

"When I was a kid, I used to make lists of what outfits to wear to school each day." I stop short of sharing that I continued this habit through most of my twenties, and even sometimes revisit it today. "It quieted my mind, somehow." Past tense.

He smiles conspiratorially. "I know how that is."

"You didn't answer my question."

"What question?"

"What kind of blue is your favorite?"

Charles smiles, *smizes*, almost. "You see that flag?" He points to the banner waving over the Elks Lodge. The logo on it belongs to his father's company; it's a grayish-navy. "That blue."

"How appropriate."

We stop at Circle and Hook for lobster rolls. I offer a suggestion. "How about we go to dinner tomorrow night? There's a great sushi place around the corner that has the best toro in town."

"Sure, that'd be great."

I take this for a plan. I should've known better.

The next afternoon, hours before our planned outing, I receive a text from Charles:

I hate to do this, but I'm really not feeling well. I just got my face lasered and my stomach hurts. That's what usually happens to me when I get my face lasered, and not just a small part, but the whole thing. I look like a lobster, probably like one of the ones we ate yesterday before it was seafood salad. Anyways, I hope you don't hate me. I'm currently accepting all forms of sympathy, including care packages, gift baskets, and good old-fashioned cards. Sincerely, Papa Lobster

Odd. A few thoughts cross my mind, including:

You couldn't have let me know earlier?

That's really disrespectful of my time.

If you've had this procedure before, why did you agree to meet me today?

I reply with:

I'm sorry you're not feeling well. I hope you feel better!

We meet again the next day for what has become our two-or-three-times-a-week marina walk.

I can't resist asking. "Have you had that kind of procedure done before?"

"Yeah, at least once a month." He sips his rosewater fizz.

"Well, we could have had dinner another time. I wouldn't have minded."

"But I wanted to." It's always about him, isn't it?

"Well. In the future, I'd appreciate a little more of a heads-up. Can we agree to that?"

"We can do whatever you want."

"I'm serious."

"So am I."

He says these things so genuine and forthright in the moment. I learn quickly that his actions speak louder than his words.

"I am very deliberate with my words. I realize not everyone is like that." I will confront him weeks later, after interspersed instances of flakiness. Pastries are meant to be flaky, not people.

"You're in the right profession."

I hate it when he does that—that cute, coy, verbal sparring. It makes me giddy. I don't do giddy.

I do manage my boundaries.

Chapter 7
Diana
2007

Rogers Gardens, an upscale, outdoor garden and gift shop in Corona del Mar, California

First Date

"What do you think of this California succulent?"

Charles crouches next to what appears to be a lotus masquerading as a water-storing genus. He caresses what I think are the petals of this cactus-like flower with a gentleness reserved for the most brittle of material.

I've never seen him more attentive to any other living thing, ever—which I guess doesn't account for much, since we only just met.

It's sweet, though, this passion of his for plant life.

It's also odd that his security detail hovers from afar as we promenade about the gardens.

"Mum insists. It's an inheritance thing." Charles will inherit his family's real estate empire in due time. "She'd prefer it be later, rather than sooner. There's nothing wrong with being safe, is there?"

I assume this is a rhetorical question.

I've lived in Newport my whole life, but I've never been here—Rogers Gardens. It's a healthy blend of foliage, fancy pots, and filthy-rich ladies of the house, and there's a soothing comfort that accompanies the fresh air and extra sunlight. I'm used to darkness. The house I grew up in, though spacious and airy, harbored shadows of palm trees that hid both morning and evening light. I could see the moon from my room, though. I learned to love by the moon. But the house was cold. Stone, gray, manor-like. There was no love there.

I've never been on a real date before, either. Most of my life, I friendzoned any guy that wanted more. I guess I've always thought I'm emotionally screwed up. And Charles was so obvious, chilling on his bale of hay like some honky-tonk beach cowboy. Yet, here we are.

"The flower is beautiful, Charles. What is it called?"

I wish he'd take some interest in me. If he showed half as much interest in me as he does in this California succulent, we'd be planning a wedding already. Not that I'm expecting anything. It's only been five days since we met. I've always wanted a fairytale wedding like the ones the Disney princesses got: Sleeping Beauty, Cinderella, Snow White, Jasmine, Ariel. I grew up thinking it was a rite of passage, like first communion or eight grade promotion. There would be lots of white roses, lots of lighting: candles, string lights, and fireworks. I would have six bridesmaids and at least two wardrobe changes: a dress for the ceremony and a dress for the reception, and maybe even a dress for our send-off, where we ride into the night in a vintage roadster. But I'm open.

At least this garden is magical. Even in the winter there are full blooms, and the curators are wizards with wisteria. Thank God Charles bought out the space for the day; I can see cameras peeping through the shutters by the entrance. It's way better than other times; mostly when I'm alone, it's so much worse. I don't mention it to Charles. I don't want to bother him with it. He's got a lot more on his mind that takes priority over my insecurities with the press.

After meandering around the rose garden and documenting the afternoon with a photo in front of the living wall, we enjoy a late lunch at Farmhouse. I have the Farmhouse vegetable plate and Charles the sea scallops, shrimp, and mussels over linguine. I've been instructed not to eat carbs in front of him. The security guard, Pablo, enjoys his own meal from the next table. He's on his phone the whole time.

"Isn't this fun? I could do this every day," says Charles. Surely he's alluding to spending time with me and not the plant promenade we've participated in for the last two hours. But to be honest, I'm not so sure.

"It's a great space, Charles. Thank you for sharing it with me."

I don't think he hears me.

Little Corona, a semi-private public beach in Corona del Mar, California

In addition to the steep, somewhat paved, ramp-like walkway that drops off its pedestrians at Tower 4, this gem of a beach leaves me breathless. A little enclave tucked beneath Ocean Boulevard, only the wandering types would know of its whereabouts. If you know, you know.

Molten, black rocks contrast deeply with the surrounding shoreline, creating a near-volcanic landscape I can only imagine resembles Vesuvian ash. Pools of sea life float in and out with the tide: anemones, urchins, crabs. It's our own private aquarium. At least, for now.

There's a tiny stream that flows down from the ravine, splitting Evening Canyon from this side. I was told once that it was polluted with chemicals and to stay away from it, and so I always jump over it, but it feeds into the ocean, so I guess it can't be that bad. The messaging is confusing.

I used to come here as a kid. That's how I learned about marine life. My favorite part was when the waves slapped the side of the rocks and would spray us with whitewash. I think I'd still enjoy that. It's another world down here.

Now, we're lounging under multicolored umbrellas that resemble a circus big top, red and white. Charles has popped a bottle of champagne, Veuve. "To our first date," we cheers. I hide my sandy feet beneath a beach towel; I haven't had a pedicure in days. My yellow sundress looks the part, but I wish I wore something that covered more of my body. The sun is disappearing and a chill shivers my spine. I pull the beach towel over my legs.

Charles doesn't notice my chattering teeth. "Did you know Little Corona is a great spot for divers? These reefs are spectacular and a great launching spot for diving." He certainly loves his fun facts.

"No, Charles. That's really interesting. Do you like to dive?"

"Me? No, no. Much too risky for this bag of bones. I'm more of a land animal." He nods pensively towards the horizon before continuing, "Do you know what *Corona del Mar* means?"

Great, he's quizzing me now. I took French in high school. I'm not sure what I was thinking.

I smile mischievously. Every woman has her secrets.

Thankfully, he responds like I expect he would, like the intellectual, Stanford-educated Phi Beta Kappa that he is. "It means *Crown of the Sea*. It is a majestic place, isn't it? A living fairytale. How lucky are we?"

The luckiest.

We're then still in silence, aside from the waves rolling and the splashes that slap across the reefs armored by barnacles. The umbrella is no longer serving its purpose, as darkness has fallen. We're half-laying, half-sitting not two feet from each other. I wonder why he hasn't kissed me.

Curious, I shift my body so that he has a sensual view of my décolleté, accentuated by my shoulder wrap. It's my only visible body part, besides my face.

Not several seconds later, he's gone. Vanished. He must've murmured something in his haste, but I didn't hear anything coherent. All I see are bits of sand covering the beach towel where Charles laid.

What just happened? Did I do something wrong?

Shortly thereafter, Pablo is beside me, taking in the view from atop my elongated neck and cleavage meant for Charles. I cover myself immediately.

"Don't worry, Miss Diana." He's dismissive, yet supportive of my embarrassment. "This happens all the time."

Somehow, knowing this doesn't do much to dull the sharp pinch of shame that holds my heart hostage. It will last until the next morning, when Charles will text me as if nothing out of the ordinary had taken place.

This happens all the time . . .

Chapter 8
Charles
2007

She probably thinks I'm a total spaz. I can't blame her, though. She doesn't have all the information. If limited to the details she knows, I would probably have the same reaction.

One of pity. One of confusion. One of disrespect.

I do wish to tell her. Only, it's too soon. To bring someone into my world of false alarms and incessant uncertainty? I wouldn't wish this angst on anyone. There are those select few who love me regardless, and I keep them close. But no one else. No one understands.

"Why don't you try . . ."

"I've heard that . . ."

"Can't you just . . ."

I've heard it all. Anxiety is not something I wish for myself; it's an illness, maybe even a condition. To live in a perpetual state of fear, unable to relax. Insomniac sleeps. Tensions in my muscles. To wake up to impending doom that never manifests, yet my brain always has to prepare for the worst.

On top of that, it's hard to explain because, well, most of the time I don't know what's going on myself.

Often, I anticipate the worst-case scenario. What if, what if, what if. It's like living a scary movie where the killer is always behind the closet door, but then, it never is. I'm constantly preparing for something bad to happen. My amygdala is always in overdrive.

My default coping mechanism is to flee. I am a runaway train. Master of the Irish Goodbye.

The most difficult part is, most of what my brain feeds me is nonsense. That makes it really hard to discern the truth. Perception is reality, and my realities are remakes of Alfred Hitchcock movies.

I can't subject Diana to that. She won't want to be with me. Who wants to deal with a crazy person who is extremely aware of all of the things that could possibly go wrong?

"It's a beautiful day, isn't it?" I always find it safer to talk about generic things. Like the weather, the landscaping, even politics. It's when conversations get personal that the mood shifts from pleasant to prophetically apocalyptic—at least in my mind. My godforsaken mind.

This home of ours is probably my favorite. While there is a public walkway that extends the full length of Buena Vista Ave, not many people—even locals—use it very often. To me, it's one of the most underrated streets in all of Newport. A long time ago, all of the homeowners retained the services of one landscaper. He has since passed away, but at that time, the street looked like one unending pathway of curated, enchanted forest. There are still eucalyptus and oaks and shrubs galore, not to mention potted flowers that line the cement on each side. It's not as uniform as it once was, but it sure is beautiful.

We have a dock, too, where our yacht and Duffy are parked. Their names are so embarrassing. We have loungers and high-top tables and a built-in barbecue setup for smaller, more intimate gatherings. Mostly family. Very close family.

Diana radiates like the jewels that hang from that swan-like neck of hers. I almost had a heart attack at the beach on our last date. Her beauty slayed me, weaponized in the form of a bare neck and crevice of cleavage. And so I ran away.

"It's stunning," she acknowledges. "The view from your dock is one of a kind. Do you sail?"

I only sail with Camilla, but she doesn't need to know that. "As I mentioned before, I am more of a land animal. I do enjoy tending my garden. Would you like to see?" My comfort zone is my happy place. Approaching the edge of it gives me hives and other unbecoming skin conditions.

Like when she stretched out pseudo-sexually on that beach towel during our beach day at Little Corona. That sundress screwed with my mind. I wanted to stay and run away at the same time.

So I ran. Self-preservation always wins.

Sometimes, self-preservation and self-destruction are one and the same.

One day, I may just spontaneously combust. Or not. It's fifty-fifty at this point.

Dates: Diana and Charles

There are thirteen of them before the engagement:

Date No. 1: Rogers Gardens/Little Corona double-header

Date No. 2: Windsor House on the bay

Date No. 3: Taylor Swift Concert

> Charles: At least we don't have to talk the whole time. I gotta say, I dig her dance moves.
>
> Diana: *"I shake it off, whoa whoaaaa, shake it off, I shake it offffffffff!"*

Date No. 4: Catalina Weekend

> Diana: He's obsessed with the seagrass here. Will he ever kiss me?

Charles: This scene is next level. I wish I had known this sooner. So green.

Date No. 5: Santa Barbara Weekend

Charles: I should bring Camilla here. She would love the shells and rocks.

Diana: His eyes are so much like the sea. I could drown in them. I think I do.

Date No. 6: Napa Valley Weekend (I sense a theme)

Charles: She seems to be enjoying herself. Woman can't hold her wine, though. It's kind of cute. She will be fun at parties, for sure.

Diana: I think he likes me. He can't stop smiling.

Date No. 7: Dodgers Game

Diana: He looks so handsome in his Dodgers cap. Those eyes . . .

Charles: Her tits look amazing in that jersey. That body . . .

Date No. 8: Two-week European Excursion

Diana: All these cities look the same: white marble, whiter people. I'm not trying to be racist, but Europe looks a lot like Newport. The Eiffel Tower is pretty.

Charles: I didn't realize how ignorant Diana can be. It doesn't really matter; as long as she follows directions, all will be good. And she's hot.

Date No. 9: Dinner at the Windsor Residence (is this even a date?)

Charles: Really hot. I can't wait to get her to bed.

Diana: I feel like a bull in a china shop. Let's hope I don't knock over the lawn jockey again.

Date No. 10: Helicopter ride over the southland

Diana: I've never seen so many colors.

Charles: Even the sun sets in paradise.

Date No. 11: Miami Weekend

Charles: I tripped over a sea turtle after we got back from snorkeling. Thank God no one got it on camera. Diana came to my rescue without flinching. (I would've flinched; I hate blood.) She will be a good mom.

Diana: I love taking care of him. I'd do anything for him.

Date No. 12: Bora Bora Weekend

Diana: This is my favorite place to bang, hands down. So romantic. There must be something in the air.

Charles: Great sex. Gone in sixty seconds.

Date No. 13: Pelican Hill Staycation

Charles: I could see us getting married here. Or on a boat. I'll ask Mum what she thinks.

Diana: He holds my hand as we walk along the balcony overlooking the golf course and the ocean. I could do this every day for the rest of my life.

Chapter 9
Camilla
1998

Floating with Charles is like floating among the clouds: light, airy, and breathless. There's so much to see, yet all I want to do is enjoy his company.

He's not much of a sailor. Charles loosens the mooring rope before pounding his chest like a silverback, with satisfaction and pride. Only, it isn't loose enough. An opportunity for growth.

I've accepted that, just like I've accepted his all-but-impending marriage to a woman (girl?) who cannot ever and will not ever love him for who he is and is meant to be. Isn't that life, though? Tangled and toxic, with dashes of pleasure mixed in, all meant to dull the pain of doom?

I should talk. Andrew isn't exactly an ethical prince.

"You know, I saw him with Anne. They looked pretty cozy," confides Daphne, a cousin of mine who acts more like a sister. "His hand was in places it shouldn't be, if you ask me."

I'm no stranger to infidelity. Humans are amorphously amorous creatures. We touch who we touch. We kiss who we kiss. We fuck who we fuck. We love who we love.

Andrew can't take my power, even if he is sleuthing around Newport like the privileged, oat-skinned male that he is. It's not his fault he has this opportunity, this vapidly unvirtuous way of living. Don't worry, I'm not dismissing his accountability. He has plenty of people to answer to, least of all me.

Despite it all, I love Andrew. Not in the way married people might, the kind of enduring, grow-old-together love. I love him in the empathetic way, the way which, when applied in the extreme, becomes enabling. Love becomes pity, an exercise in futility. I do not pity anyone.

"I think I'm improving," Charles calls from the bow of our sabot as we navigate the tide. "I'm hardly feeling any nausea at all!"

Charming, this man is, with his unkempt hair awash in sea water from a recent jostle overboard. It was all in good fun. We weren't wearing any clothes; only dumb smiles.

"Hunny, you look greaaaaat! Now let's hoist that sail! You remember how, yes?"

Sometimes he needs encouragement. Sometimes he needs a kick in the ass. Sometimes it's hard to tell. Sometimes the only way out is through.

As we lay sunning on the sailboat, the *Lovers Corale*, we trade turns sparring with questions of intimate details and treasured secrets, the stuff of romance and tortured hearts.

"What's your biggest fear?" He's solemn and cool.
"That someone might not be willing to fight for me as much as I'm willing to fight for them." The salt air is my truth serum. "What do you want your legacy to be?" Go big or go home.

He considers this. "I want to leave the world a better place." I don't think he knows. Yet.

Our dialogue drifts, like the bobbing seagulls, towards more tangible matters, like his anxiety. Charles is receptive to my questions, my interest in wanting to understand his reality.

"Why do you give it so much power?"

"I don't give it anything. It's just there."

"I just mean, I understand you can't control when it comes. But you can control how you respond, what attention you give it. Right?"

He's quiet. It's disconcerting.

"Thoughts are like . . . songs on a radio. Some songs are good, dance-worthy, even. Others are, well, not. But you let them play on in the background while you move on with your life."

Charles turns to me, upright, his shoulders pointed towards mine. "I see your point. I never thought of it like that."

"That's what friends are for."

Chapter 10

Diana

2007

I'm not embarrassed by my family. Shaped and perhaps a little shamed by them, I am the play dough and they are my sculptors. Who else do you listen to during the most formative years of your life?

My parents loved each other, once upon a time, until their lives became embattled by resentments and expectations. We could all see it, us kids. I was often overlooked, the middle child, the forgotten mare. Michael, the prince, has only good memories. Sarah, the boss lady, has only bad ones. Me? I remember traces of nothing. That's a choice I made. We only ever get so many choices in life. I swear there's a maximum allotted to each human. It's the only sense of control we ever feel. In many ways, we're products of a system, an assembly line of outputs controlled by those with a little more power than those on it. It's always about power. Just look at Mom and Dad. Dad won custody because he has more money. Mom has money, too, but not as much, and not enough to influence the powers that govern such matters. That's the story that I see.

"Money isn't everything." Mom preaches these words, but I can tell she doesn't believe them. She's an idealist. Me, I'm a realist. I get that from my dad. I see things as they are. I just need the facts. Yet facts are facts, and it's the truth that's personal. What is truth? I only know what I know, which isn't very much. I was never a studious child, nor did I ever take much interest in the kinds of topics those philosopher-king types discuss, including but not limited to an existential view of how the world works. I get by.

"You make people feel good," my dad once told me. "Use that." It's probably the best advice he'll ever give me. This, from a man who left us with nannies after Mom moved to LA, and who would prefer to eat dinner alone. Apparently I (we) didn't make him feel good enough to prefer company to solitude.

"We're lucky," Sarah would say. "Most people don't have what we have, never can, and never will. Don't forget that."

I haven't forgotten. But I still crave things. Like touching. A hug every so often. A kiss. A word of encouragement. A smile. Warmth.

Mom is a sad person. On Saturdays, when we visited her, the tears would churn nonstop. I didn't understand why.

"Because," she would sob, "I don't want you to leave tomorrow."

How did I grow into such a warm person, when all I was ever surrounded by was cold, empty concrete and empty emotions? Maybe I'm not warm at all. Maybe that's a fallacy, a trick of my senses. I told you I wasn't that smart.

Even Mom asks about my match with Charles. She had an affair with a married man while she was living away from us. I don't know how valid her position is, given this fact. "Do you love him, or do you love what he is?" On one level, he's just a sad, lonely man who just needs looking after.

I reply, "What's the difference?"

I don't see any. Maybe I'm blind, too.

Chapter 11
Charles
2007

I should be so grateful to have this life planned out for me. To not have endured the struggle of paving a concrete path through an Amazonian forest. To not have thought twice about my future. To not have needed to choose.

What's so great about having choices? Most often they are hard. Painful. Scary. Especially if they're the right one. What kind of cruel joke is that, choosing between what's right, and what's easy?

"You will never have to choose." The Firm made sure of that. "You just have to make sure you don't screw it up."

Mum didn't mean to do that, I don't think, introduce a whole other set of pressures that don't accompany self-discovery, but expectations of success. Expectations are deadly. They're rote with disappointment, sadness, frustration. A blow to the heart. After all, expectation is the root of all heartache. She couldn't wish that for me.

"I wish you great success," she says. "I planned it that way."

She didn't plan for me to suffer. These panics, these cold sweats, these hard nights' sleeps without much sleep at all. It just shows how much uncertainty there is in the world, how much we think we can control. But it's all an illusion. A figment. A facade of a castle that looks like the most refined porcelain, but is really just plaster painted with marbled speckles. Sometimes my whole life feels like a human rights violation.

I don't even like real estate. I like buildings, market values, and money—who doesn't. But I don't want to run the business. I would never admit that to Dad. I *could* never admit that to him. The thought floods me with guilt, the shame of whatever the opposite of gratitude is. But I am *so* grateful. This conflict, this dissonance, eats me alive like a rotting carcass turned dinner for the lion's pride.

"It's all set up." Somehow that makes it worse.

Dad, bless his heart, pretends to understand. I don't share much with him about this. Everything else? Absolutely.

"You have everything." He's not wrong. "And now, you have someone to share it with." He tastes a lick of gin from his highball glass. "Diana, she's a good choice." Ah, choices. "She is beautiful. She's kind. She will be a good mother." I believe all of these things.

"You may not love her yet." Mum reads my mind. "But give it time. Maybe one day, with any luck, you will."

JOB DESCRIPTION:
THE NEXT WINDSOR WIFE
(FOR INTERNAL USE ONLY)

Should any of the proceeding content find its way into the press, corrective and punitive action will be taken on the offending party or parties. You have been warned.

SUMMARY

The Windsor Group seeks a frothy, upbeat young woman to lead the burgeoning real estate business alongside its future chief executive, Charles Windsor. The role offers the opportunity for personal appearances, philanthropy, and visibility on the world stage. Located in the glamorous coastal respite of Newport Beach, California, the job requires frequent travel and press availability, and an excellent taste in fashion.

QUALIFICATIONS

- "Newport Nautical" bloodline
- Member of a local yacht club
- Under 30 years old
- USC (University of Southern California, *not* University of South Carolina) educated
- Family net worth of at least $1M
- Preferably blonde, tall, and athletic
- Never married
- Interest in philanthropy or non-profit initiatives within Orange County

The hiring process includes several in-person interviews, a written questionnaire, and a final evaluation by the head of Windsor Group, Elizabeth Windsor. To be considered for the opportunity, candidates should send their CV, cover letter, and a current headshot and bodyshot to careers@windsorgroup.com. Serious candidates only, please.

ABOUT WINDSOR GROUP

Windsor Group is a globally recognized real estate firm managing over $100B in assets and property. Founded by George Windsor, the Firm today is run by the current family matriarch, Elizabeth Windsor. President and CEO Windsor believes in the freedom of capitalistic enterprise and the American Dream. She encourages all men, women, and non-gender-conforming individuals to apply for roles within the institution. "We celebrate all people who aspire for professional growth and profit in the real estate industry, and support our company in achieving greatness." In the next five years, Windsor expects she and her firm will meet their asset goals of $1T.

Chapter 12
Camilla
2000

These events are so apropos. Don't get me wrong—I enjoy dressing up for a ball as much as the next debutante, though I'm not a debutante.

I grew up with privilege, yes. But not as much as some of the others I shared classes and clever banter with.

I work hard, too. I'd like to say most UCLA grads do, but I'm not naive enough to think that's a universal truth shared by all Bruins. Like most humans, it probably depends on having interest and understanding, or the willingness to work at it. I don't often see willingness to work; the ease at which we can perform life makes working less valuable, less distinctive, less laudable. Why work if the reward is diluted by so-called benefits algorithms and AI?

Estate planning law is hard work. Squabbles and stellar accusations (many of which are proven to be true, on some level) are part of the job. Wealth doesn't insulate people from pain. While it may be dipped in gold, pain is pain. Just ask the emperor about his new clothes.

Fundraisers, on the other hand, are an excuse to get dolled up and momentarily forget the clichés that govern societal expectations.

"It's for a good cause!" is the epithet cooed by many a development officer soliciting the next big donation check that buys a table of ten and their name on the program under "Gold Standard." My firm occupies one of those coveted spots. My boyfriend insists we go to show our support, but mostly to show our faces amidst the active members of Newport society. Andrew is a criminal attorney. We met in law school at Brown and found our way back home. He went to the high school across the bay, but we never crossed paths—until one of these loathsome events three years ago.

"They always remind me of how we met." He thinks he's being romantic. I think he's being cavalier. But I love him anyway.

His family expects us to marry, but I know better.

"A match made in marital heaven," chants his father, also a criminal attorney. They work at the same firm. Nepotism never lurks far from Newport nobility.

We'd probably be content in a marriage. It would certainly be one of convenience. Marriage really isn't about the people in it, is it?

It's about everything around them—the family, the duty to legacy, the commitment to ensuring that legacy remains intact in the future. It isn't about the union between two people. It's about the contract between two histories joining forces for a promising economic tomorrow.

"You look like a million dollars, babe." Speaking of money. Andrew never skimps on the high praise about my ensembles. This time, it's a sparkling Givenchy gown with teal and blue hues. I look like an expensive peacock. I can't remember the last time he complimented my brain.

"Thank you, hunny. And you look dashing as ever." Truly, it's always the same: suit, tie, and loafers, with the obvious variation in color combinations. It must be boring to be a man.

After he picks me up in his Lamborghini, we speed through the mere mile to the Harborside Pavilion, the venue hosting the evening's festivities. A tribute to Newport's past, this building overlooks one of the largest small yacht harbors in the world: the Southern California Riviera. It's exactly what it sounds like—Monte Carlo without the racecars.

Even for an ENFJ like me, these fêtes have their cap on fun. I usually check out after the silent auction. Sometimes the programs themselves drone on for hours. *No one is here for the program,* I think. I'm sure everyone else is thinking it too, but no one has the balls to enact a change in protocol. Classic groupthink syndrome; a recipe for ostracism. No wonder they say change is bad.

"Thank you all for coming." The radiant boom of a baritone signals the start of what is sure to be the most riveting program in the history of hospital fundraising. I'd recognize that baritone anywhere.

I catch a glimpse of him as Andrew pulls me by my smaller-than-average hand towards our table in the center of the room. Table 8. Proximity is everything. Location, location, location.

He's dapper in a navy blue suit, accented by a silk shirt in robin's egg blue. I always told him he looks good in blue. It distracts from the sadness in his eyes, also blue, but more like ice than water.

"Your sadness is temporary," I'd tell him, hanging off the bow of one of his many yachts. It might even be a fleet. He's not one for sailing; I taught him how. "It's not who you are. It'll pass, and you will be happy again, because you are a happy person. Don't forget that."

I've never pitied Charles. That's not what he needs. He needs a friend.

I know the minute he sees me. His face softens and his shoulders rest at attention, with structure, yet relaxed. The kindness in his eyes shines through, melting from frozen water to a rippling river, alive and flowing.

After his introductions, Charles takes his place with the rest of the board, who are required to eat their meal on stage like some kind of performative display of what it looks like to "make it" in Newport.

Sipping soups, knifing filets, toasting triumphs. Unattainable, yet completely ordinary.

He finds me on the dance floor afterwards, my favorite place. Andrew has just gone to get us drinks. As soon as my side is vacant, Charles appears, bearing two glasses of Veuve and the stupidest grin I've ever seen.

"I thought he'd never leave your side." His words are pure of heart. "I was plotting a murder so he'd have another matter to attend to."

"'Another matter'? Is that what I'm reduced to? A matter of fact?" Wordplay, my vice. Sometimes my savior and sometimes my sin. I hope my body language betrays my feelings, for my words are my armor. I'd be naked without them.

"You matter more than any of it." And he kisses me, right there, for all of Newport Beach and their patrons to see.

For once, I don't care about any of it—this pomp that's full of circumstances so many of us can't control. Even for those we can, we falter at the behest of something stronger: power. What is control, if not a badge of power?

My circumstances, in this moment, are not all that ideal. But I can't control that any more than I can control the feelings I have for this person, this man, whose family has all but chalked me up to a fellow Newportite who's not quite Newport-y enough. What is *enough*?

So I kiss him back. It's been ages since our lips have locked, maybe even years. But our connection has never faded. Not since that dinner party where we met, where we stole away from the airless cheers and jeers toasting a birthday girl; the party that ended in a contentious fight with her cheating husband, all but launching the most bombastic of divorce proceedings since Brad and Angelina.

Instead, we toasted each other. I remember that night often—not for what happened, but for what didn't. We didn't touch. We didn't flirt (well, maybe a little). We didn't make any promises.

"How do I taste?" What a ridiculous question to ask.

"You taste like solace." I was honest.

"You are my solace." He was assured, if not completely absentminded of his actions.

We dance a little, following our likely abhorrent display of affection. After all, this is a ball, and dancing is the center of it.

Andrew comes back maybe ten minutes later—enough time to live a dream and destroy another. Gentleman that he is, Charles takes his leave and my champagne. I'm buzzed a little, but not enough to dull my senses.

I sense Andrew's body in my arms, rigid and tight, so unlike Charles. He wraps his elvish fingers around my waist with pressure such that my ribcage constricts involuntarily. He then pulls me closer so that we're hip on hip. What's gotten into him? This is not the form for dancing amongst this group. He surely knows that.

"You seem rather fond of each other." Andrew's words are sharp, like the point of the fountain pen he uses to sign his most important papers.

Of course he saw. I shouldn't be so naive. Everyone saw.

"He's just a friend." It's the truth.

He pulls me in tighter. "He must be a really special friend."

The next morning, when we wake up in bed to the sounds of the foghorn that signals the weekly crew race, Andrew proposes.

"I've thought a lot about this." How left-brained of him. We're in our matching pajamas, barely facing one another. I notice the ring box sitting atop his nightstand, a foreboding vessel about to unleash its contents. "I think we're a smart match, you and me. I think we will be great together. I think we belong together."

I give him credit for the *we* statements. It's the *I thinks* that make me wary.

I should be thrilled. At the very least, flattered. I am neither of these things.

I am amused.

"If I say yes, will you promise to love me?" As if that's the most important thing.

He considers this with silence, a bitten lip and wrinkled brow. "I promise."

In the end, it's good enough for me.

I nod my tacit compliance, an acceptance of my fate as the future Mrs. Bowles.

Andrew retrieves the blue box once belonging to Pandora, now a symbol of our union, our future, tethered by twine and tortured hearts. I know his secret. All the better. The question is whether he'll reveal it or keep it.

I open it. A sparkler, yes. Simple, round, so unlike me.

"It's five carats." He slides the princess-cut diamond onto my finger. It fits. Or does it? The platinum band is elegant and clean, as I expect our marriage to be.

Unattainable, yet completely ordinary.

Chapter 13
Diana
2008

He seems especially nervous today. Is it me? Maybe my neckline is too deep; a capital V.

The shoreline echoes with the rolls and rumbles of a swell shaking the sand. Berms create sea cliffs, jagged yet soft as they wrap the curves of the shore. Daylight hovers over the horizon, parallel to the pelicans that sweep in their flying formations. Also a capital V.

Charles carries a picnic basket consisting of champagne and sandwiches, the perfect afternoon snack.

"Why don't we sit on the tower?" he suggests. "A different perspective."

The peninsula is empty this January, aside from the onlookers who turn into sunset peepers and swell sightseers. Typical of a tourist town. We're away from the traffic that takes over pier parking lots and Balboa Bar stands. We're away from the noise, the commotion, the bastion of carpetbaggers that collect coins outside Sharkeez.

"Homelessness is a real problem." I've mentioned this a few times. "Something should be done." I want to do more for a cause. For some reason, I don't imagine he'd support such an act of philanthropy.

"We focus on hospitals and healthcare, not homelessness." He's crude and self-centered, but what single thirty-something man in Newport isn't?

Today we're wrapped in a wistfulness I otherwise can't describe, stitched by the thread of duty, responsibility, family. Rules; so many rules. And yet, aren't rules made to be broken?

I fit into his yacht club world, yes. The pageantry. The pomp. My blonde hair blends with the rest of them. Bombshells, I think they call us. They, society's commentators, sit and snarl in their press box of judgement, observing the players and analyzing their movements. All for the sake of wrapping the game and reporting on its highs, lows, and prospects for the future. It's all speculation. Can't they see that? No, not through the foggy lenses of their rose-colored glasses. It's real. But then, perception is reality.

Charles is wounded. He needs someone to take care of him. I think I'm her, that person. I love him.

Clad in cutoffs and a billowy peasant blouse, I climb the adjoining ladder and splay myself on the lower platform. My feet dangle near his chin. He can see down (up?) my blouse. I'm not wearing a bra.

He smiles up at me, yearning and desire dimpled in his cheeks.

"I think we should get married."

Are you asking me? I shiver. Could this be real, this romance? That's what this is, isn't it? A gesture of hearts, smothered in salt air. Salt air that stifles the senses and numbs all thought. It's gaseous gaslighting.

"Will you marry me?" I see the ring pinched between two fingers. It's pretty, but it's not me. It has a gold band. The diamond must be at least six carats. I really don't know for sure. Classic, sophisticated—I am not these things. But I am the future Mrs. Windsor. Or so it would seem.

Since he's asking me to, I must choose: a diamond ring, or loneliness. At times, they might be one and the same. I knew as a child I'd always marry someone in the public eye. I just didn't know it'd be *the* person everyone in this town, in this world, is after.

"Well, of course, darling." After all, It isn't really a question. This life, this future, is meant to be. It has to be. "I love you." I leap into his arms, and the six feet from sitting on the tower platform becomes an embrace. My hands find his cheeks and I kiss him, a peck on the lips, before he slides the engagement ring onto that finger. I squeal with excitement, dropping L-bombs like it's D-Day. He nods his head as he does, exhaling in some sort of relief.

His reply?

"Whatever love means."

Chapter 14

Charles

2008

She's happy. At least, she seems happy. I'm glad. Truly. She deserves to feel happiness.

Her sister, Sarah, was always the chatty type, filling voids with loud noises. A dramatic girl. That's why it didn't work out between us.

But Diana, she's a swan, where Sarah is a squawking seagull chasing tourists. When we dated, Sarah betrayed me. I don't know how else to put it. How does one expose the bones of one's personal relationship with another? She didn't do it for money; as far as I know, there was no money.

"He's kind of a snob," Sarah was quoted as saying in the most salacious gossip column of the Newport Nauticals. "He doesn't hold my hand in public and avoids large gatherings unless he's absolutely required to attend, you know, for his mommy's business. I don't think he gives me enough attention. His priorities are him and himself alone. Maybe his mum. Who wants to be with someone like that?"

Even if a fraction of those claims are true, what gives her the right to smear the name of someone whose company she keeps? Willingly, I might add.

I'll never forgive her for those trinkets of betrayal. "You've just done something incredibly stupid." There was no way to coat it in sugar; we're not two kids sharing a packet of Fun Dip. We're adults, navigating the norms of an insular society. We both know this.

I would never make such a mistake.

She's redeemed herself, though. Not enough to absolve her from all disgust, but at least I no longer view her as a pile of crap. Women can be like that—sweet on the outside, bitter on the inside.

"Will Diana be what you need?" I appreciate the concern of the local socialites for my happiness, although past precedent might indicate they feel nothing but contempt and jealousy for the next Mrs. Windsor. The pretty one. The kind one. The one with a big heart (and bigger boobs). "She could disappoint you. You might end up hating her."

But it's okay for you to hate her? I always wanted to ask. The things you despise her for are things she cannot control. Perhaps this is a human flaw relegated not only to the worst of us, but also to the best of us.

"I can't guarantee that." It's true. I would tell them, "I promise not to betray her the way you betrayed me." I can't help it; it's how I feel. When is honesty ever bad?

People surprise you, even the morally bankrupt ones.

Just ask them.

And now, we have a wedding to plan. I'm not one for the finer details of place settings and Chantilly lace; that's Mum's department. And will soon be Diana's.

Diana will make a fine wife, like Penelope, and Melania, and Hilaria. She has the cache, the charm, the blonde hair. A never-married woman with endless potential for photo ops and philanthropic appearances. She's much better at it than me. I pretend not to notice. When I'm angry, I shame her for it. She should know better.

No one ever said this life was easy. Or fair.

Just ask me.

Chapter 15
Camilla
2000

I'm not a coward. It's none of his business, really. We hardly know each other.

It's been weeks, has it? Not enough time to declare feelings or faith in a future together.

I enjoy Charles. This is no secret. His self-deprecating and moody charm touches me like the hand of a wanton angel. "Your laugh, it tickles my soul." Who says that but Charles, the heir to the empire real estate aficionados could only dream of? I don't care about that. I can take care of myself.

Andrew is the suitable choice. Confident, cunning, and just a little too bossy. A partnership made between two people, linking two families, two finances, and two fragile egos. The proposal was anything but romantic, and the wedding even less so. A recipe for a happy marriage.

"You look radiant." Did I? It's the best thing to say to a woman donning sparkles who really wants to be wearing lace. I love lace, especially floral-inspired lace. Yet there I was, shining like the Chandelier Bar in the Cosmopolitan Hotel. Dangling crystals chimed about my body, from my dress to my earlobes to my too-much tiara. Andrew's mom insisted on it. She's related to a duke somewhere in Europe.

I lived through the day as though I was watching my own life from across the bay, on a bridge, waving to the newly wedded couple in celebration. We shared our first look on the dock outside the Bay Club. I held my bouquet of peonies and eucalyptus, the one thing where I insisted no compromise be made. Whereas salt air is my truth serum, flowers are my soul. I will not compromise my soul.

"You look radiant." I'm sure the sun hit me—me, really—in such a way that it stole spectators away. The power of an artisanal ball gown: I'm reduced to a limp mannequin holding flowers, and the dress wears me. But I smile even still. *Grin and bear it,* I think that's what they say. Everything is temporary, including this day of ritual and really expensive champagne. They're serving Dom; only the good stuff for Andrew Parker Bowles and his new wife.

Wife. For a while, I didn't think it in the cards for me: the ball-busting, outsmart-opposing-counsel attorney. I'm not exactly the poster child for femininity. I sail, I write, I deplore big business and even bigger bank accounts. But here I am, literally fraternizing with the enemy, or one of them, at least.

It's the responsible thing to do.

Charles will understand.

He'd do the same thing.

The banquet hall twinkles with the lights of the harbor beyond, the intersection of indoor and outdoor living that is so typical of Newport. It's a study of etiquette and manners: who sits where, who arrives first and last, who can leave the table without explanation, and who cannot. It really is beautiful, in a *deep sigh, how did we get here*, kind of way. A system governing manners and matters, of the heart and of the hearth. My heart is lonely today.

"A toast to my bride." Andrew never misses an opportunity for the spotlight. This is the first of six speeches on our wedding day. "A vibrant, endlessly hopeful rose of a woman who always keeps me smiling. I am the luckiest man."

Word choice is an interesting thing. It's as much about what one chooses to include, as what one chooses to exclude.

"A toast to my groom." I laugh at parallelisms that are cheesy and overused. "A winning, salaciously sexy magnet of a man who always keeps me guessing. I am the most grateful woman." No one in the room knows what *salacious* means. And so they clap, jeer, and cheer, clinking glassware in symphony before seeking out another opportunity to do so. This domino effect of drinking leads us deep into the night, through the first dance, the last dance, and the In-N-

Out truck parked in the alleyway. A double-double is the only thing I eat all day.

For five minutes, I'm alone in the dining hall where Charles and I first shared sparrings over sea bass chili. I don't recognize the feeling at first, the hollowness: part empty, part full, all vacancy. Growing up, I set the example. In my default position as the oldest of three, I blazed the trail. I share this trait with Mom and Dad; we relate across and through time and space.

"You'll figure it out," Dad empathizes.

"Happiness is a choice," Mom chastises.

They make a good pair. The most loving partnership, if there ever was one, that also happened to build a life of privilege and promise, of freedom. Not a fairytale. No glass slippers. No spell-breaking kiss. It's better. It's real.

I cry a little. For what they have, and what I don't.

Tomorrow will be better.

Chapter 16
Diana
2008

It's abysmally dark by the time we arrive. We pull up to the back, the front entrance to the guest house. There's a roundabout that deposits entrants at the top of the walkway that leads towards the front door. I notice light fixtures—lamp posts from modern England like in the *Peter Pan* cartoon—that adorn the perimeter. But they're not lit.

It's cold. It reminds me of my childhood home, which happens to be a few communities away, called Spyglass Hill. I can't see much in the dark. Maybe it's darker because of the shadows that overlap the night.

"There's no one here," I wonder aloud. Stu, the driver, responds with silence. He's a Jason Alexander type. More *Seinfeld* than *Pretty Woman*.

They knew I was coming. It's been planned for days, my move into the household. I didn't even want to move in, but Charles insisted. "I won't have my future wife living separately. What will people think?" As if that's the most important thing.

"You'll meet the staff in the morning, I'm told." Stu unloads my suitcases. It's more information than I received. "The master is up the stairs on the left." After delivering my bags inside, Stu leaves me alone with my thoughts. They're sad, and tired, and a little bit anxious. It will be better in the morning.

"And this is Maria, the House Manager." A woman called Rosie completes the introductions of the house staff. They stand, attention-like, as if during morning roll call in the barracks at Camp Pendleton. The sun spills onto the bamboo floors behind them, creating shadows without any definable geometric shape. Because of this, it's difficult to see the details of their faces. Half-light, half-dark. I don't know what this room is called. It looks like a museum.

I'm not even sure who Rosie is in relation to the group. She's obviously more senior and supervisory. She wears a skirt suit, navy with the most pin-like of pinstripes. It looks expensive. She has a No. 2 pencil tucked over her right ear, and her hair is swept into a low bun just above the nape of her neck. She belongs in the front of a military school classroom.

"Hola," Maria squeaks. I'd expect a more commanding presence from a staffer called House Manager. But this is new to me, so what do I know?

I know the staff—Arbella, the lead housekeeper, Chad, the head chef, Cici, the other housekeeper, and Stu, the driver I met last night—have likely met several women with whom Charles had now-latent trysts. But I can only imagine. They seem nice and real.

Rosie leads me into the living room following the staff's dismissal. The snow-white couches are too pristine for sitting. "There are several more staffers that you'll see around the building." Rosie is matter of fact in her delivery. "They're not worth meeting. High turnover, you know."

No, I don't know, and now I'd feel stupid for asking, so I don't.

"Typically, Charles will rise by 7 a.m., help himself to a slice of avocado toast, prepare for the day, and be out the door by 8:30 a.m. at the latest. Rupert will leave out a few clothing selections for him to choose from in the master closet. What he doesn't wear will be put away by Cici."

I don't know who Rupert is. I didn't meet him this morning. I don't ask.

A youngish woman walks in just then. She's wearing khakis and a navy blue-colored shirt with a whale on it. Apparently the uniforms mimic that of the private prep school down the street.

"Perfect timing, Claudia." Rosie is commanding yet harmonic as she waves her hand towards this maybe-employee with a come-hither wave. "Diana, this is Claudia. She will be your personal assistant. Whatever you need, she will help you with."

I stand to introduce myself, extending my right hand in her direction. That seems like that the right thing to do.

"It's not necessary, Miss." Claudia's deep voice stuns me. Such a baritone from such a petite person. "You can tell me what you need after you and Miss Rosie are finished. I will wait in the closet."

I will wait in the closet? "Uh, um. Oh, okay. Nice to meet you."

She leaves us with a curt nod. She must be a lesbian. No judgement.

"Do you have any questions, Diana?" I notice Rosie doesn't attach an article to my name, as she does with *Sir Charles*. I sense an attempt at a *fuck you, Princess.* But what can I do?

I have so many questions. *How do I get my car? Am I allowed to drive my car? Where do my clothes go? How do I get ahold of Charles' schedule? How does he get ahold of my schedule? What time does he come home? When do we see each other? What fork do I use?*

"No, Rosie. No questions." I wonder if the rest of the staff holds the same opinion.

Claudia is folding my several pairs of jeans when I enter the master suite. I didn't notice when I arrived, but it appears the whole right side of the closet is dedicated to my use.

"You'll be wearing a lot of clothes," Charles has said. "Like it's your job."

I've worked as a kindergarten teacher since graduating from USC. I love children. They are the future. But Charles has made it clear it's time for me to abandon that career path in favor of supporting the *family business*. For me, that means wearing the latest fashions and appearing on his arm at philanthropy events. I don't know what my role at home will be. I assume we'll have kids. I'd be pretty involved in that, I'd imagine—you know, since I will be entirely responsible for the birthing process.

My wardrobe is already hung, displayed, or folded as Claudia finishes tucking the last pant leg into a drawer. "Hello, Miss Diana." She nods her head as she did before, curtly and with too much decorum. "How can I be of assistance to you?" Her look is earnest, yet contrite. I wonder how she came to be a Windsor family staffer. Sometime I will ask her. For now, I want a friend.

"I feel so alone, Claudia." I figure appealing to her humanity would be a good place to start. "I don't know where Charles is, and I don't know what I'm doing in this house. It's overwhelming." I stop short of tears. Crying makes me uncomfortable, and I wouldn't wish that on a perfect stranger—even if she is paid for *other duties as assigned*.

My tear ducts are barren wastelands, and Claudia doesn't bat an eye. But she offers something more, some wisdom. "There is nothing worse than living in fear. Be brave, even when you're afraid. The only way out is through."

I wonder what kind of experiences she's had that might provoke such insight. She can't be more than twenty-five years old.

Claudia continues, "Each morning, I will leave a few outfits for you per Mum's direction. Your selection is on order and will arrive soon. I will make sure your breakfast, lunch, and dinner are prepared to your liking and in a timely manner." She hands me an iPad. "Use this to rank your preferences so I can optimize your options." It's like a digital personal shopper for my Windsor life.

"Claudia—" I'm not sure of the right way to ask this. "How do I get through this?"

She smiles at me, half sad, half hopeful. "Just breathe."

Chapter 17
Charles
2000

Women always betray me. Even the one I've come to call a really, very close friend.

I cried when I heard. Not trout tears, but the bluest of whale tears. Excessive blubbering.

"I know you feel pain," drawls Mum, the empath, "but it's time to move on. Camilla clearly has, and you should, too."

I heard about it while I was away on business, in Tibet, no less. It couldn't have happened long after the ball. The ball where we kissed. The ball where we professed how much we mattered to each other. Does any of it matter now?

She knew I could never marry her. "An act of defiance," as my father would call it—anything that counters the way of the Windsor clan. She's a Bruin. She's brunette. She's "ethnic." She's not Newport Nautical.

So why am I so distraught?

She got me. She didn't give two shits about it all. She found humor in our relationship. She never pitied me.

Her reaction to my despair?

"You never would have married me anyways, Charles. Why does it matter who I marry? Or, for that matter, why does it matter that I marry at all?"

She's deft in her logic. "Why are you marrying?"

"Because it's the responsible thing to do."

We share many values, Camilla and I. A sense of responsibility is one of them.

"Sometimes, I feel wholly unlovable. It's a symptom of loneliness." I know, because I feel it too. "I figure marriage is the next best thing. At least I have someone to grow old with."

Damn her and her thoughtful observations. It's one of the things I enjoy most about her.

"I am happy for you." But also, I am very, very sad.

Some things are better left unsaid.

Chapter 18
Camilla
2016

Damn him and his insufferable need for me. This lust. This sycophant to society masquerading as a homely and devoted husband. His loquaciousness often leads to the seeding of a love nest on the south side of Laguna. The Ritz, if I had to guess.

Is it need? Want? An unsatisfiable desire for power and control?

It's treason, this haunting of halls that are supposed to be ours. I smell their perfume. I taste their breath mints. He thinks I don't know.

Until today.

Andrew hides his tracks well. He carries a broom to sweep the evidence under the proverbial Persian rug that sleeps in our entryway. His entryway. I don't know. It doesn't feel like mine.

Most days, we get home within minutes of each other. On the days he's off affairing, he scuttles in by 7 p.m., in time for dinner. It's 7:02 when the French doors open today.

I'm sitting in the parlor. It's obnoxious that we have a parlor. I prefer to call it the den. Same purpose. My desk overlooks the water of the canal with its still, muddy waters that sometimes produce a rotten egg smell. I moved in after we were married. I should've moved in before. Maybe things would be different. I planted rose bushes along the perimeter for a pop of color. I like my desk; it's a Victorian writing desk with the original finishings, including an inkwell. It's the most thoughtful gift I've ever received. It's not from Andrew.

"Hey babe, I'm home." He trots into the house with the gait of a man who just got laid: slightly limpy and slightly steadied.

"How was your affair?" In my mind, I channel *The Graduate*. I don't have the patience to be subtle. He continues into the kitchen for his nightly whiskey.

"The meeting was long." He can be as dense as any man.

I emerge from the parlor, unphased by his choice to be coy. "You mean to say, she rode you so long your dick nearly fell off?"

Mid-sip, Andrew licks his lips like a predator tasting a fresh kill. "Something like that."

"I figured as much."

"Now it's your turn."

Before I can breathe, I'm naked in our modern farmhouse kitchen, leaned over the quartz countertop, moaning thrust by thrust. It feels good. It always does.

That was never the problem.

I finish first. He climaxes, not in me, thank God. He knows better.

We stare at each other, taking in each other's' nakedness. Exposure.

"This is how it's going to be. You know that. You always knew that." He's calm and terse.

I'm not surprised. I'm disappointed. Which, to be honest, is worse.

Surprise, that's unexpected. I cannot honestly say I didn't expect this.

Chapter 19

Diana

2008

"I'm really confused."

I say this often, I've noticed. I've adopted it like one of those fad terms like *bro, lit, if you know you know*. Only it doesn't feel like a fad. It's my new normal, my always state of mind.

What's worse than being confused?

I'll tell you.

It's when they see you confused and don't do a thing to help you be less so. When they revel in your revisionist fairytale gone awry. Your pain becomes a spectator sport, and you're the ball in play, being battered around like the object of gamesmanship you are. Because that's your role. Nothing more, nothing less.

I am the literal object of their disaffection.

Charles keeps himself busy with work, or so he says. I believe him, mostly. Camilla doesn't seem to threaten us in any meaningful way. I may be younger than them, but I'm not blind. Even if they were to carry on as they do, I'm the future wife. I have the power.

Even if I don't.

Still, it's far too early to give in. I'm not a tampon, one-time use, gross and disposable.

"They gaslight me," I confide to Grace, a member of the circle who seems more real to me than the spray tans of the other WAGS.

"What is this 'gaslight'?" She's in her fifties. I guess she didn't get the memo from her daughters. I can't believe she has daughters. She looks like she just graduated college. I should know, because I just did last year.

"Gaslighting is when someone makes you think you're doing something wrong, or that something is your fault, when it's not at all." That's a really confusing definition. "It's basically mind games."

Grace reapplies her petunia-pink lipstick, rubbing her smile into a submissive straight line. "Maybe it is your fault?"

I hadn't considered this possibility. I'm apparently so caught up in my problems, I might as well be wearing red-tinted eyeliner. The puffiness is harder to hide. My esthetician has practically given up on me. "My fault? I didn't do anything." I sulk like the schoolgirl who gets in trouble for minding her own business while a brawl ensues a few feet away. Culpability by proximity.

"Could that be the issue?"

I can't tell if she's trying to be helpful or if she's completely uninterested in my plight. "What should I do?"

She's not listening to me anymore, so wrapped up in her own world of wonder and warfare. Her husband is very publicly conducting an affair with a princess from somewhere in Europe. For some reason, it's always Europe. Perhaps Grace isn't the best choice of confidante, though I do admire her sense of place. She knows he couldn't do without her. She plays by the rules and makes him sorry he ever started playing the game.

The other women pity me. I can tell. I hear them.

She doesn't know what kind of dress to wear.

She eats before it's time.

She always orders the wrong drink.

These rules are arbitrary in the application. They achieve nothing. There is no goal they support meeting. There is no victory to be had in playing by them. There is no trophy to hoist after winning them. There is no winning. Only losing.

The photogs are merciless, camping outside my house even before I moved into the Windsor estate. I was on my own, without help. Camilla would call Charles complaining of the four outside her place. I had thirty-two. I didn't mention it to him.

"I'm tired," I say to no one in particular. It's more of an observation than anything. More and more often, I find myself observing my body as an entity separate from me, from Diana. I see myself from afar, looking into this life built by society. Isn't it a funny thing, how society isn't a person at all? It has no body, no brain, no soul. It's a fiction, a figment of our collective imaginations to which we assign power. Who decides this? I definitely didn't.

"Perhaps you should take a rest." Jodee, a neighbor from around the corner of the Windsors, appears at my side like an apparition-turned-flesh. "Here, let's go to the balcony."

The balcony is a paradise accented by Italian string lights aplenty. Luscious foliage scales the wrought iron that frames the space; there's barely any of said wrought iron visible, the ivy covering it as much as it climbs it. Our view is a black blanket of velvet with fireflies sewn across it, a mimicry of the night sky on a clear night. Sometimes it's hard to escape the light. The best place to stargaze is in the desert, away from home glow and streetlamps. I want to be there right now, in the silence. Away from the teeming hive that is society.

"Sit here." Jodee is delicate in her command, more instructional than directive. "Take off your shoes. The blood flow to your feet is probably nonexistent."

Obviously she's done this a time or two. I peel off my Manolos from the heel. They're beautiful in their red soles; they remind me of finger-painting. Very expensive finger-painting. My circulation returns toe by toe. "Thanks," I mutter. I have no intention of being rude. I am, as I said, tired.

"Tricks of the trade." She sips a few times from her glass of wine, a deep red, perhaps a cabernet. I've learned as much from my sommelier instructor. Why I should be called upon to know every varietal of bottled vine is beyond my comprehension. The Windsors insist upon it—a "family legacy." But I know not of this legacy, and I fail to clarify the lineage. Perhaps I just don't care.

"Sometimes it feels like a never-ending trade negotiation." Of course, I'm referring to my upcoming marriage. How corporate it all sounds. What would a divorce even look like? Not that I'm anticipating it; I've lived it. I've seen what it does to families. It's like a termination following a soured manager-direct report relationship, accompanied by a handsome severance package. Who wins?

I didn't mean to bring her into my personal issues. Charles won't like that. So I shut up and sit in silence. She watches me, like a puppy perplexed by the antics afoot.

Jodee places her hand over mine, the one that's hanging over the fancy bench we're sitting on. Fancy only because it's ivory with abalone-trimmed uplighting. The hand she uses boasts a stunning sapphire ring, accented by what appears to be yellow diamonds.

"Don't worry, sweetheart." She drinks what is left of her wine. "It will all get a lot worse."

Petra, my press manager, loathes me. Ever since we met, she's had this unfriendly vibe. I mean, she's not supposed to be my *friend*, per se. But tilting the outer corners of her mouth *up* every so often wouldn't kill her.

"No posting without permission." Outside of our introductions, which consisted of a quick hello in passing—Petra was dousing a PR fire—basically everything this woman says to me begins with the word *no*.

No texting. Paper trails are evil.

No phone calls to unauthorized people. Wiretapping is still a thing.

No outings unless otherwise approved by the Firm's scheduling department.

I don't understand how a whole department could be devoted to scheduling.

One afternoon, before an appearance at the winery, we spend what feels like hours in Petra's office reviewing the "Windsor Way," as she calls it. Her presence intimidates me. Sitting poised, yet leaning over her West Elm desk and matching chair, her outfit consists of a high-waisted chiffon skirt and fitted blouse, each in shades of blue and darker blue, respectively. It softens her otherwise-sharp facial features. Her nose is narrow and her eyes are so emerald, they could be mistaken for that very green parrot from the Isla Tortuga. She's equally as smart as she is attractive. No wonder she's single.

"Every public moment is planned. Your job is to execute the plan." Petra gives no wiggle room for mistakes. In her last PR job, where she led press relations for the Capulets, I heard she made the lady of the house cry every day. Something to do with a rule Petra has about no boat rides unless it's on *Invictus* or *Aftermath*. The woman used to love her boat rides, but now suffers from panic attacks any time the word *boat* arises in conversation.

I haven't even tried asking her a question. I probably should, but I don't want her to think I'm an idiot. She makes it sound so simple, so foolproof that a monkey could do it.

I feel like a monkey sometimes. *Dance, Monkey, dance!* A lobotomy doesn't sound so bad right now.

"No *press*-ure." Petra is funny, but I'm uncomfortable with laughing. For some reason, I think she might find it offensive. So I smile and process the information as best as I can.

This is what I understand:

The press and the Windsors have some kind of informal agreement regarding their relationship, which basically amounts to what levels of access they do or don't get. I hear that the press reports extensively on the family's events in exchange for that access. Given the thirst for any news about the Windsors, including their business and the family, the relationship has been lucrative for the media and important for the family, too. Some powers that be have speculated that the Windsors have overextended their empire and may be approaching the beginning of the end of their legacy. At least, that's what Claudia has shared with me.

"It's the easiest way for them to stay in the news without betraying all their secrets." Claudia mentions this to me casually while we're dressing for a charity golf event. She helps me into my

Lilly Pulitzer frock and zips me from behind. "It's genius, if you ask me."

Genius. And they picked me. "Petra calls the Windsors 'The Firm' sometimes. What does that mean? The business?"

Claudia shakes her head as she hustles to my vanity to retrieve eyeliner and mascara. "The Firm is an informal title for the Windsor family and its many companies, including the staff that keep the business functioning."

"So, basically . . . all the family members and everyone that supports them and the business?" That seems extensive.

"Yeah, that's the gist. There's the real estate holding company, the family office that runs the household and manages the family's homes, the 501(c)3s for their charity work, the partnerships in other stuff they work on . . . it goes on and on."

My mind is blown. "And that's all considered 'The Firm?'"

"Uh huh." Claudia's distractedly crimping my hair. I trust she won't burn me with the wand. "Charles' grandfather came up with the concept. Supposedly he once said, 'we're not a family, we're a firm.' And it stuck."

Wow. *We're not a family.* That sounds intense.

I guess that makes sense . . .

"It looks like the Rogers Gardens holiday room on steroids."

Sarah's not wrong.

The entryway to the pavilion twinkles in that cascading pattern reserved for those willing to pay top dollar for such an effect. It can be troubling, the costs associated with building a timeless, tinsel-lined stage. That's what this is. At Christmastime, everything is amplified, including the decorations and the drama. A stage, and all the men and women merely players.

Shakespeare had it right.

"We should stand over here, away from the step-and-repeat. I've been photographed enough for a lifetime."

She's so dramatic. And likes to pretend she's more important than she actually is. No one even knows who she is. She's a wannabe, like the Spice Girls song.

I love the oak banisters in this space. It reminds me of the cabin in Big Bear we used to visit as kids. We'd spend weeks up there in the winter, chasing snowstorms that left the mountains covered in white powder.

Sarah owned those slopes back then. She cut glass with her skis like a serrated blade to an ice sculpture. I was lucky if I made it down the mountain safely. Once, my cousin Alison and I ended up on a blue diamond run in Sunday River, Maine. We'd fallen behind the group, the two less-experienced skiers that we were. East coast mountains are an entirely different animal. The west coast is the best coast in every other way. Thank God we were together. At one point, I soared down a run, free and unwavering in my confidence, until I veered left into a thicket of really tall trees, landing on my back with my skis overhead.

I laughed before I cried. Not out of pain (thankfully, I didn't hit my head), but out of shock.

We walked down the mountain after that. Sarah never lets me forget it.

Sarah outdid me in everything. Then, we stopped living in the same household. Then, we stopped being compared to each other. Then, we started building our own identities. Then, we started clashing.

"That dress looks kind of baggy on you. Did you lose weight?" A diss, disguised as a compliment.

"I'm trying to. Thanks for noticing." My gown is yellow, similar to the one Kate Hudson wears in the movie *How to Lose a Guy in 10 Days*. It captures the light well, sort of like the shimmer on the ocean when the sun has set. I'm even wearing a diamond necklace, a canary diamond like the one from the movie. I think she's jealous of that.

What do I care? I got the guy.

Even if it's only out of convenience. Minor details.

That's the thing with modern sisters, I've noticed. Not brothers, not siblings—sisters. It happens particularly with sisters close in age, maybe under ten years. Somewhere along the way, while we were each building our own identity living our own lives, we lost respect for each other while finding ourselves. Why can't we have both? She doesn't understand my life, and quite frankly, I don't understand hers. But I don't treat her differently for it. At least, I don't think I do.

As we walk together, linked at the arms through the decorated hall, the foreign and familiar commingle like apples and oranges in a fruit bowl. I see members of the press with their phones held up like tape recorders once were, shuffling around, speaking on and off the record with various guests, I imagine hoping to scoop the best headline for the evening. I see members of the family milling about as they always do, pretending (or maybe not pretending) to be important.

"For all this money, the bacon-wrapped scallops should be bigger." I don't disagree with this observation.

I really like the floor-to-ceiling windows, though. This space is my favorite property by far. I can see the ferry traversing the harbor, steady and reliable. I can see the mountains framing the foreground of islands that make up this town. They'll disappear with the sunlight soon. It's easy for me to remember how much I love this place, standing here, overlooking the simple elegance that shaped its history.

But then the lights go down. A spotlight finds Charles, awaiting the commencement of this year's Christmas toast. I'm supposed to be up there with him. I'll probably get in trouble.

There's your headline.

Chapter 20
Charles
2008

Boston, Massachusetts

Beacon Hill reminds me of England. The cobblestone streets, the lampposts standing like sentinels, the tightly wound corners where blind spots are a way of life, rather than an inconvenience. Makes sense, though. After Philly, this town is as British as it gets on American soil. Just look at the State House.

I arrive just after sunrise. I prefer to spend the night sleeping rather than waste the day in the air. After a few business meetings, I'll take in a game at Fenway and go to bed early, not before taking a stroll around the Public Garden. I have a soft spot for the Swan Boats and the Make Way for Ducklings statue that they dress in sports apparel during respective postseasons of the hometown teams.

The Hub has spirit.

We have stuffy yacht clubs and too many blondes.

Diana seems to be adjusting nicely to Windsor life. "Where are you going?" She peppers me with questions as I, or rather Rupert, packs my suitcase. Thank God we timeshare a plane. Checking luggage sounds like a logistical nightmare. She probably just forgot to check my schedule with Rupert.

"Boston."

"For how long?"

"Two nights." Shouldn't she know this?

"Okay, travel safe."

For some off-putting reason, I get the sense I've forgotten something. Laptop? No. Paperwork? That's not it. Wool socks? Rupert always remembers my wool socks.

I'm sure it'll come to me.

A week later—Kauai, Hawaii

"It's only for business, dear. You'll be so completely bored, it would just be a waste of time. Why don't you go to happy hour with the twins?" Diana has been pouty lately. Not in the cute, teenage way that she can be when she's trying to initiate foreplay.

She balks at my suggestion with the fire of a thousand blazing arrows from one of those war movies I can't remember the name of. "Why would I go to happy hour with your twin cousins who hate me and think I'm a joke?"

"Don't be so dramatic. Just because they're models and thinner than you doesn't make them less than human." What's wrong with stating the obvious?

Clearly Diana harbors an unconscious jealousy. At my reply, she slams the Victorian doors in my face and races off to the movie theatre, probably to watch another episode of *Breaking Bad*. If that doesn't scream insecurity, I don't know what does.

She doesn't even like Kauai. "I prefer Maui, myself. There's more to do, more people around. Kauai is like sacred space. I feel like an invader when I'm there."

I'm saving her from this interloper mentality. She should be thanking me, not forsaking me.

Me, I yearn for the garden isle. Our compound is nothing to sneeze at, either. It's a gentle irony that the gardens here inspire my own gardening efforts at home. There's nothing more satisfying than pruning a Mr. Lincoln rose bush that, a few months later, produces the most perfume-y blooms this side of the bay. Tending a garden is like tending a child, where nature and nurture intersect in a fusion of life. Obviously children require more than sunlight, water, and choice clippings from time to time, but I envision the metaphor holds up in the macro sense.

The helicopter views of the island are spectacular, especially Ha'ena State Park. Camilla prefers Hanalei, but it's a little crunchy for me. There's a food truck scene.

"When will you be back?" I don't get why Diana doesn't ask Rupert these questions.

"Three, four nights tops."

"Okay, travel safe."

A week after that—San Francisco, California

"Why don't you want to spend time with me?"

"It's not that I don't want to spend time with you. I have responsibilities. There are places I need to be. Don't you understand that?"

She should know better. She grew up like this too, with duties and commitments and binding protocols that may not be written, but might as well be etched in stone. Rosetta's complement. Are we making a mistake?

"What I don't understand is why you don't ask me to go with you."

Honestly? I've never thought about it. Dad never travelled with Mom on her business trips. He always worked from home and spent time with, well, me. It didn't occur to me Diana would have an interest. Even if she did, would it make sense for her to travel with me when there's a wedding to plan and a home to make?

"Trust me, my dear, I'm only thinking of you. What would you do all day in SF, anyway? It's the most boring city in the world. Wouldn't you rather lounge by the pool or go shopping at South Coast Plaza?" That even sounds better to me, quite frankly.

"Well, let's see. There's Golden Gate Park, the beach, hiking..."

"You can do all those things here."

"But I won't be as close to you."

It's sweet, the way she pines for me. I am a lucky man.

But for some reason unbeknownst to me, it yanks me back. Like one of those slingshots pending release.

I'm still held back. When will she let it go?

"So? You won't be as close to me. I won't be gone long."

"But we're engaged. I want to spend time with you. Isn't that what engaged people do?"

"What?"

"Spend time together."

"Not when one of them is about to take over the biggest real estate empire in the world."

"So business comes first."

"Yes."

"Always?"

"I don't know how to answer that."

When she walks away, I swear I hear her crying. I didn't see her face, so I don't know for sure.

There's nothing to cry about. I hope she doesn't do this in front of Mum.

Chapter 21

Camilla

2008

"Do you enjoy yachting?" I figure it's the least heinous, most honest way to ask Diana if she does enjoy the sport. I don't have anything to hide.

"I actually get seasick." She wraps her supple lips around the rim of her champagne flute. Her mimosa disappears in one fell swoop. She must be thirsty. "It's more of a blanket motion sickness. I get sick in cars, too. And airplanes. It's really unfortunate, to be honest. It makes travel feel more like a job than something fun. And I love to travel."

Good. Boats are still my domain. "Charles isn't keen on sailing either. He goes when I beg him, but hardly any other time. Unless for an appearance or if someone valued with a lot of zeros asks." I figure she knows this, but in the interest of friendship, I offer some affirmation. It's best she trusts me than not.

We trade turns spearing our ahi poke over lunch at Nobu—Newport, not Malibu. Good thing it's already seared. If it were raw, we'd have matching bloodbaths on our respective plates.

I change the subject. "What's it like to be engaged?" I mean specifically to Charles. I know what it's like to be engaged. Perhaps her experience is different than mine.

"It's—" she pauses, holding the *S* like a hissing snake. She doesn't realize she's doing it. I'm caught in the blinding sandstorm that is her inner dialogue. I chew my poke with intention. Savor the flavor. Savor the moment.

Diana finds her words. Or perhaps they reveal themselves to her in the midst of the hide-and-seek game between her mouth and her mind. "Lonely."

Lonely? I reach for my water to keep my hands busy. I wait for her to elaborate.

She doesn't.

"Oh? How so?" Three syllables should be enough to continue this wormhole of a conversation; too long, too thin, too narrow.

"He's never around. He's always travelling for business. He doesn't call, he doesn't text . . . much. He just seems . . . so far away from me."

I'm hearing a lot of "he." We all project. Where's her accountability in this?

She continues without prompting. Thank God. "I've never been engaged before, let alone in a serious relationship. Maybe I'm just being dramatic."

Ah, introspection. How refreshing.

"How many serious relationships have you had?" I fork some microgreens in sesame dressing before she answers.

"Actually, none."

I nearly choke on my kale. "None?" It's all I can manage between chomps.

Her eyelashes are absurdly long. She must have extensions. "I've dated. I went on dates. But mostly they ended up not going anywhere." She shrugs her shoulders. "I friendzoned most of them."

So she's never been in love? I can't ask her that. I don't want to know the answer. Instead I go with, "I can understand that."

Diana sighs a little. "How did you fall in love with Andrew?"

A surprisingly thoughtful question. One I've never answered aloud, or for myself, if I'm being honest. "It was easy. I'm a sucker for charm. He knows his place in the world. And he doesn't need me. I think that's most important."

"He doesn't need you? And that's good?" Her puzzled expression betrays her innocence.

"Exactly. He doesn't need me. He *wants* me. That is so much better."

She doesn't get it.

"Need is about survival. Want is about choice. Andrew chooses me every day." It's true. Even in his infidelity, he chooses me. "And I choose him." Not as true as I'd like it to be.

I catch myself. What an interesting reaction.

"I choose Charles." Diana is assertive in her claim, bold in her voice, yet timid in her truth. While she is sure of herself, she's not sure of him. So she thinks.

Really, though, the thing she's not convinced of is her choice to marry the man we both love.

"I know you do, dear. Now, let's order dessert."

Chapter 22
Diana
2008

"Wear a hat, just in case." Charles knows I've never worn hats in my life. Not the kind of hats generally associated with the Kentucky Derby, at least.

I don't own any hats. Just baseball caps for when I work out. I'm sure that's not what he meant?

Why should I hide? I'm not a dirty secret. Still a secret, I suppose.

We're on our first public outing since the engagement. It's a Lakers game. Of course we would be photographed. What good would a hat do?

"It's best to wear a floppy one, so that you can tilt one side over your face should you need to hide yourself." Claudia mimics the gesture she's describing with a jut of her hips, like one of those

Venus figurines you learn about in school. I've come to like her. She defies convention within the convention. I strive for that much, if not more.

"Why, though?" It seems like a half-assed attempt at anonymity. It still doesn't make sense to me. I'm beginning to think it's not supposed to make sense. Maybe I should update my whole outfit. I thought a Kobe jersey and skinny jeans would suffice. I guess our job is not to attend as fans, but as representatives of the Windsor Group.

"It's not your job to ask why. It's your job to *be* the why." That should be stitched on a throw pillow for the lounger in my dressing room. I will need to be reminded of this, I can tell.

Children always ask why. Am I a child? No. I'm a grown woman, looking for direction and support. The *why* would help me infer what to do, and more importantly, what not to do. it's a missed opportunity. It's not like there's a handbook I can consult as a reference about these things.

Perhaps I should write one.

We decide on a black, billowy blouse and black leather motto leggings, paired with chunky ankle boots, also black. I appear to be in mourning. Aren't I, though? I'm mourning the life that once was, and will never be again. "They'll balance well with the hat." The hat dictates everything. Just as rules do.

The car, also black, arrives promptly at 5 p.m. to collect me. Stu informs me Charles will meet us there. "He will be arriving via chopper shortly before you." Why didn't I know that? I am always the last to know.

Am I expected to wear my hat in the car? It sounds silly that I should have to, but I don't want to mess up my hair.

I wear it the whole drive, just to be safe. I will ask in the morning. (No I won't.)

Charles greets me at the lobby entrance of the Ritz Carlton at LA Live. His chopper lands on the helipad atop the hotel. Sometimes I wonder if this is all really necessary. Who is he trying to avoid? How much easier does this make his life? While I'm new to this world and its rules and regulations, the overblown antics are hard to miss.

"Great outfit, dear. You nailed it." *Finally.* Some sort of recognition for my efforts. They're not even my efforts, exactly. Well, they're my efforts at making an effort to not screw up. Screw up what, exactly? I'm still trying to figure it out. I'm somewhat glad I didn't take my hat off in the car. "How was the drive?"

It's a pretty safe bet he's forgotten I experience motion sickness, literally from any kind of motion, but now doesn't seem like the appropriate time to bring that up. I will make a mental note. "Good. Stu is . . . an efficient driver." We arrived in under an hour, which is magic considering LA traffic. Changing the subject. "Ready for the game?"

The first time I notice his cuff links is when he's holding my hand as we're escorted through some not-so-secret tunnels under the grid of downtown LA and into the arena, at the arena level, where access is limited to staff, players, and apparently, special people like us.

My stomach tightens. Do I say something? I should say something. "I like your cuff links, babe. Are they Tiffany?" I squeeze his hand for encouragement.

He flinches instead, hardly a promising reaction. Our hands detach like torn mesh metal. It's messy, and phalanges fly everywhere. "I believe they are, yes. Thank you for noticing." Charles pecks me on the cheek as we continue our route around the concourse to our courtside seats. "We'll be in these seats for a quarter, then head to the suite to greet clients. At halftime, we'll decide to stay or go."

I nod my tacit compliance. "Honey . . ." I can't stand his lack of clarity. Surely he knows this. No one likes secrets. "Who are the cuff links from?" My tone is even. At least, I think it is. How is one supposed to know when her mind races like sabots during a regatta?

"I don't remember, sweetie. I think they were a gift?"

"There are two Cs on them. Could they stand for Charles and Camilla?" My voice is still even.

"I think they're Chanel, but I guess they could." liesLies my soon-to-be-husband tells me. "Is that a problem?"

Coy cover, Camilla. He doesn't get it.

"No problem at all."

Chapter 23

Charles

2008

She doesn't seem mad.

She has no reason to be. Aren't gifts, especially accessories, meant to be worn? Camilla is a very good friend. The best friend, actually. She'd be my best man if she was, in fact, a man.

Am I the asshole that doesn't get it? There's got to be a Blogger thread I can consult about this. Surely I'm not the first man in the history of the planet to piss off his fiancée because he's wearing something another woman *gifted* him. It would be a shame for such beautiful, wearable artwork *not* to be worn.

"Here we are." Finally, we're at our seats next to the Lakers team bench. Jack Nicholson nods me hello. Kobe points to me. Good. The important people know we're here.

That's not true. Everyone is important. I'm just being a schmuck.

"These are... wow." Diana, impressed by the proximity to the action, loses her words. She's not great with words to begin with, not like Camilla. Where Camilla is a wordsmith, Diana is a locksmith. She holds tight to her feelings. It's very difficult to ever know what she's thinking.

So I ask her. "What do you think?"

I'm referring to the seats, obviously.

"I think you're having an affair with Camilla."

A choice moment, in front of every broadcast network camera, to tell me what she is thinking. "That's ridiculous." I'm smiling for said cameras. "We're very good friends. We have a special friendship."

"Yeah. Friends who fuck."

"Can we talk about this later?" My face burns a shade of fuchsia that won't show well on screen.

"Whatever suits you, dear." Eerily cool, she slips her hand through my arms so we're linked together like chains. "We're in this together."

Chapter 24
Camilla
2008

I was always the go-to.

"Camilla, watch your brother."

"Camilla, take out the trash."

"Camilla, where's the lemon slicer?"

We had an understanding, my parents and I. They were both born the oldest children in their families, just like me. We share this experience in life, this first lieutenant of a rank. It's not good or bad, it's just what is.

I never resented it like some people might. I owned it. I still own it. Guess who Mom calls when she needs advice? Guess who Dad calls when the markets are out of whack and he needs a sounding board?

I grew up sailing. A survival skill in a town equal parts land and water, it was the sensible thing to do.

Sensible. Ah, yes—the sensible choice.

In life, we are often cast into roles we cannot control. They are beyond what we've planned, and in some ways, even more inhibiting because we do not accept them as fate. What is fate? Genes predispose us to our realities. We cannot control these cells, these fundamental units of life that comprise our existence. To think we can is some mad-scientist nonsense.

But we can control ourselves. How we respond. How we behave.

When Charles and I are together, I am at peace. I am calm, I am crippled by hope, emboldened by fear.

His hand grazes mine, unintentionally, of course. Our proximity would afford for such opportunity. It has several times now.

"Sorry," I utter quickly. That's my default reply.

But something changes. "Actually." I declare my position. "I'm not sorry. I like touching you. So I'm not sorry about it." In case it wasn't clear. You never know with these silent types. Charles isn't silent, really; he's just not a sharer. Unless he wants to be. I guess that's distinctly human.

That's the leader in me. Dormant for most of my youth, I've learned to rise.

My parents would tell you otherwise.

She was always a leader. Blazed the trail. She just didn't think of herself that way.

I guess it makes sense that I became an attorney. I like to ask questions, poke holes in logic for fun. Now I do it for a paycheck. But it's more than a paycheck. It's peoples' lives. These disagreements—over estates inclusive of houses, more houses, boats, airplanes, jewels, koi fish—these are the things that make up peoples' lives. The memories. The moments. That's what I'm fighting for. It's not really a fight, though maybe to the opposing parties it is. But that's not my role. My role is that of adjudicator, to optimize opportunity for my client. Usually my opponent is the court system. I don't feel bad exposing the system for its abhorrently outdated legislation around who gets what, what the taxes are, and who loses. There's always a loser. This is America.

"Camilla shines when she's presented with a situation that seems un-figure-out-able. She always figures it out." That's what Andrew says about me. God love him for his candor, even if it's this quality of myself that he admires but also detests. A double-edged sword, like most meaningful things.

Like words themselves: both a tool and a weapon. Modern media weaponizes words every day. Some call it news. Some call it propaganda. There's always an agenda.

I love words. I get frustrated sometimes when people don't know how to use them, or misuse them, and I can't understand what they're saying. Like in the SATs. There's a whole industry built around tutoring students to "master the test." It's not about assessing your aptitude for vocabulary (among other things, obviously); it's about learning the language of the test and measuring your ability to do that. And the language is in English, using English words. It's all very confusing. An existential dilemma in many respects.

Most people don't understand my musings. I generally keep them to myself. It's lonely sometimes, in my mind.

I confide in my mom, my best friend. She doesn't understand many of the out-there ideas that swim around in my brain and really don't get much oxygen. But she listens, bless her heart.

My biggest fear? That I will never have anyone in my life to love me like she does. Andrew isn't that person. I know it; he knows it. And I accept it, but I don't like it.

The things we do for love.

Chapter 25
Diana
2008

"Sarah." Between sobs, I realize I sound like a wailing foghorn. "I don't know if I can do this."

It's the truth, awful as it is. Despite my love for him, this ridiculous Rochambeau of rules hangs on every cell of my body. The body that I'm supposed to nourish, but treat like a punching bag for my angst and depression. I am depressed. No one sees or hears my calls.

I don't use words. Words are senseless things. No one listens. Actions speak louder than words, isn't that right? I am acting on my body.

"Di." Sarah sits on the edge of the master bed, which is coated in the silkiest duvet from the latest American designer. It's a bed of comfort. I need comfort now. "You're just getting pre-wedding jitters. Everybody has them. It's very normal to feel this way."

Normal to feel like my body is eating itself alive just so it can survive a day dedicated to ritual? A wedding isn't even about the marriage itself. It's about everything that surrounds it.

"I am so unhappy." I don't know what else to say. Words fail me again. "I'm alone in this nightmare, and Charles doesn't help me. He helps Camilla."

"Maybe she needs more help than you do."

I consider this. Maybe? "But I'm his future wife. Shouldn't that mean more?"

"It should. But that doesn't mean it does. And quite frankly—and I say this with all the big-sister love possible—I think you need to be okay with that and move forward."

Sarah was always one for zingers. It's one of her boss lady traits.

"And," she stands to smooth out the comforter behind her, "the place cards have already been printed. It's a little late to change your mind."

The place cards, yes. What a waste it would be if they never saw the event they were intended for.

Is that what my life amounts to? A printing inconvenience?

Sarah meanders over to my dressing table, a beautifully ornate vanity built in the Tuscan tradition and imported from Italy. It was a gift from one of the major winemakers, I'm told. "Don't you want this?"

This. "What is *this*?" I process her question as I speak aloud, hoping that bringing the words into the world will clarify their meaning. It doesn't.

"This life." She dabs on some of my new Chanel lipstick, a natural pink. I still prefer Bobbi Brown, but Mum insists. Windsors aren't showy, Sarah says. Their opulent standards of living excluded. "This life of luxury, comfort, stability. Don't you want those things?"

"I could still have those things without Charles." It's a fact everyone seems to overlook but me. Why is that?

"True. But not to this extent. This is the top one percent, Di. It's unlikely you'd get another offer as good as this one ever again."

I don't really understand this fascination with the top one percent.

Sarah continues, "If the United States has 325 million people in 160 million households, according to the IRS, that means 1.6 million households fall into the one percent category. If we're talking about the world as a whole, according to the Credit Suisse Global Wealth Report, the world's richest one percent, those with more than $1 million, own 44% of the world's wealth. Their data also shows that adults with less than $10,000 in wealth make up 56.6% of the world's population but hold less than 2% of global wealth." As always, it depends on who you ask.

It's not like we grew up poor. We're from Newport, too. Our address may not be Harbor Island, but our parents built their own legacy, even if it pales in comparison to the Windsor estate.

Sometimes I forget my baseline is skewed compared to the rest of the world.

"Funny how offers are non-negotiable. Especially with no prenup. Isn't that ironic?"

She's not listening. "Maybe. Irony doesn't mean a thing. It just means two or more circumstances happen simultaneously that may or may not have anything to do with each other."

"What if they do?" I'm dying to know her answer.

"What if they don't?" There are always at least two ways a situation could go, or three, if you include the status quo. Which is, in fact, a choice.

Risk. That's ultimately what it comes down to. I thought about asking for a prenup, even though it's simply not the Windsor way, according to Mum. I have assets, too—just not as many as my betrothed. Honestly, I'm a little embarrassed to ask. They'd mock me. Accuse me of compromising their trust, or something.

Chapter 26
Charles
2008

I don't know if I can do this.

Well, I can. It's in motion, and inertia isn't so full of friction. We're on cruise control.

It's the responsible thing to do.

I couldn't do that to her, to Diana. It would ruin her, leaving her now, after all of this. The engagement has been a tour of tiaras. She's been a good sport about it, but I don't understand why she nags me when I fly for work or come home after the expected hour. It's to be expected.

Not all things go according to plan.

"Don't be foolish, Charles." Mum is both angel and devil incarnate. Somehow, she always has both sides in mind. She's a

Libra. "You know better than to entertain feelings about this. It's not about feelings. It's about family. It's about the Firm."

Mum had some hard choices to make in life, many I'm not privy to. I do know marrying my dad was a scandal. For years, her parents had planned for her to marry a man called Felix. He came from oil money. I don't know what happened, exactly, just that Dad wasn't the family's first choice. Something about a Greek/Danish/German ancestry. World War II complicated things. "It was very hard for me." She hides her pain, but it glimmers in her eyes. "I wouldn't wish that for you."

"But you worked it out."

"Not without sacrifice." She's stolid now. "Not without pain. Not without loss."

I'm a simple man. At least, I'd like to think so. I understand duty. I understand responsibility. I understand obligation.

I don't understand love. What it does to people, how it vexes the senses and turns us to mush. I don't like mush; it's messy, shapeless, and not useful by any means.

Diana loves me, she says. She looks at me on the pedestal I was born to stand on, the pedestal that is my past, my present, my future. She recognizes my sadness and accepts me for it. She allows me to be me. Who wouldn't want that in a partner?

"I understand she's the suitable choice." Diana checks all the boxes. At this point in my life, not many can. I acknowledge that is my own doing, a reflection of my preferences to fuck around in my twenties. As a product of modern America, I don't see the problem with this approach to a bachelor life.

Then Dad got involved. "It's time."

My dad is many things. An orator is not one of them. The fewer the words, the more serious the matter. I knew it was time to move forward.

Sarah and I had a good thing going. Then she ruined it with oversharing. Some people can't balance public and private life in a way that protects yet promotes us in the appropriate way. It can't be taught.

Diana, we believe, has this. She's sweet, and kind, and knows when to leave the limelight. She doesn't overstep. She shines in her silence. That's how we prefer it. That's how *I* prefer it.

"You may not be happy." Mum shocks me with her sentiment. "But you will live well. There will always be pain. But you will have less."

At what cost? Sounds like it could be expensive.

I think it, but I know better than to vocalize it. Speaking it makes it real, and I'd much rather live in this fantasy than in any alternative I'm not aware of.

Chapter 27
Camilla
2008

"I understand more about why these things happen, but I'm not sure I'm okay with it."

We stand here under the lights of neighbors' homes as the darkness grows darker. The glow wraps around us like a warm blanket. I feel heat, triggered by the intensity of the moment, though my hands burn with cold from the crispy night air.

I have puppy nose.

"I think you're really brave," I tell him. I did. I do. His strength, though riddled by pain, is apparent to me tonight. Charles rises, despite the opportunity to hide. He could've erected his shield and hid me from his pain and from himself.

But he chooses not to. I see strength in that. I see hope in that. I see truth in that.

"I don't want to be alone, but that's my mental illness working its magic. I don't mean to push away people and hide myself away. But I can't control it until it passes."

I don't realize he's crying at first.

"You can cry in front of me whenever you want." His vulnerability pleases me. This man, so imposing, sharing himself with me, confirming my suspicions of his full heart. I don't take pleasure in his pain, no. But I take pleasure in his choice to be real with me. How could I not be honored? An act reserved for the smallest segment of one's personal circle, especially for a man.

I wish more men would cry openly. Society deplores it. Our expectations of men are just as fucked up as our expectations of women.

I embrace him, fling my arms around his torso, reaching behind until they connect and interlock. He's much bigger than me; my head rests comfortably in the valley of his chest. "Both arms." He resists me at first. Then he gives in to the peace.

We trade turns sharing whatever we feel compelled to say.

"I have dormant feelings for you. I haven't entertained them because I don't know where I stand. I don't know how you feel about me. I think we're friends, but I'm confused."

He never confirms or denies his feelings for me or otherwise.

"You say when you're with me I help your mood and anxiety. Wouldn't that mean you want to spend more time with me?"

"But that's not what I'm thinking when I'm in the middle of it."

Ah. Tricky.

"The best relationships I've had are with women who are more bullish."

I don't know if I am or can be bullish. I'm just me.

"Sometimes things come to a head and it's time to share the tough things."

"'To a head'? That sounds like the beginning of something bad."

"No, no, it doesn't have to be a bad thing. Sometimes things are better on the other side."

"Like today. Like the clearing after a snapshot of a rain shower. What a great metaphor for the day."

It was a great day; the boat parade. The double-candy-claw win of sour worms and jelly beans. The waxing crescent.

He's neutral about the moon, but I find mystique and meaning in it. We were both born under a waxing crescent.

"There have been many times where I could have walked away." He speaks of now-tenured friendships. "But I stuck it out, and they turned out to be the most fulfilling of my life. I know from personal experience it can be hard. But it was worth it. I promise you it will be worth it."

He says I've been really patient. If only my family could witness this revelation. I'm patient when I want to be.

"I think you're really brave." I say it many times.

"Bravery has nothing to do with it. I don't think I'm brave. I think about the people who support me and I don't want to let them down. It's not bravery."

I understand. "It's love."

"Yes." He sighs in affirmation. "It's love."

I know it then. He loves fiercely, those he chooses to love—this sensitive soul who once told me he's a lover, not a fighter.

His shell of sarcasm cracks that night. Inside, I find the gooey interior of a man who lives in a world defined by the absence of control, a control beyond his own he doesn't have the power to overcome, yet. A soft, sweet center, like a butterscotch square. That's when I know I can love him.

"I promise I won't abandon you." My intentions are good.

I'm not sure I'll be okay with it.

Chapter 28
Diana
2008

"At least your legs look great!"

I know she's just trying to help. But being the centerpiece of the *Stars, They're Just Like Us!* spread in this weekly rag isn't helping my induction into the family.

Claudia and I critique the arrays of photographs while she makes the bed and I overbrush my hair. My hands need to be occupied; otherwise, I may cause myself physical harm accidentally on purpose.

"Petra is going to have a cow."

As soon as the word *cow* verbalizes, I hear the clack of stilettos echoing through the marbled halls.

I brace myself for impact. *3 . . . 2 . . . 1 . . .*

"Dianaaaaaa!"

Oh, shit.

"We're in the bedroom, Petra," I say with as even a tone as I can. I sound like a squeaking mouse.

"Hold your ground. Remember, you're the soon-to-be-Windsor, not her." Thank God for Claudia's reminders. I can't help but think she's at least somewhat amused by these exchanges. I've seen her indulge in way too many gossip magazines.

I inhale deeply as I continue brushing my hair. It's so long now, like Sleeping Beauty's. I wish I was sleeping right now.

"What the hell do you think you're doing?" Nice to see you too, Petra.

"Please don't speak to me like that." It's all I can say to assert my pseudo-power as a future Windsor.

"Can you explain yourself?" My efforts are apparently pointless. She wears a snarl where there should be anything but.

"There's not much to explain." It's the truth. "The press wanted a photo, and they wouldn't leave the school until they got what they wanted. So we negotiated one photo."

I pause before continuing. She shows no signs of empathy or sympathy—maybe apathy.

"One photo, and they agreed to leave." I anticipate her next accusation. "I didn't know the sun was directly behind me. I forgot what I was wearing."

It was a conservative look, a sweater vest pulled over a button-down. It was the skirt that caused the media sensation. It was white, that was the mistake. It had a print of hearts all over it.

"Don't be surprised if it's remembered as the iconic skirt moment." She's threatening me. "Now, if you'll excuse me, I have some damage control to take care of." Petra floats away, furiously tapping on her phone screen. Only she could float in a flurry.

I could give two shits what she thinks. What am I more concerned about?

What will Charles say?

"I think it's time you stop working at the school." Charles speaks simply and to the point, like the businessman he has been groomed to be. "Time to start your next role."

His reaction wasn't as bad as I thought it would be.

And yet, all I can think is, *Why does this feel like the beginning of the end?*

Chapter 29

Charles

2008

"Getting married on a boat is bad luck."

Thanks, Eddie. "Some best man *you* are." I've never been one for boats, but Mum insisted. "Just make sure you don't lose the rings."

Nerves abound in my insides. These aren't butterflies. They're oversized pterodactyls headbutting each other in some Jurassic cavern underground. Only inside me.

"As long as you don't fall overboard, we can consider this evening a success." my brother Andrew speaks from the absence of experience. Ignorance? He hasn't been married yet.

The boat is a masterpiece, though. A complete vision of a yachtsman's wet dream, down to the details of the teak wood accents that line the galleys and basically all surfaces and countertop equivalents. A double-decker vessel composed principally of fiberglass, there's nowhere to hide, even in private.

"Is that a . . . jacuzzi?" Andrew points to a smaller boat floating beside us, something like a thirty-footer, passing by.

It does, in fact, have a jacuzzi built into the back end, enclosed by glass and steel. In it are five almost-naked women (girls in their twenties) scream-singing to Jay-Z's "Ball So Hard." There's probably a line of cocaine somewhere on the deck.

"We should invite them aboard!" Eddie, my other brother, ever the advocate for inclusion. He gyrates so vigorously I fear his hand might fly off from too much roof-raising. Generational differences.

"What we should do is toast the man that bagged the most beautiful woman in Newport." Andrew comes to my rescue. The three of us form a triangle, three points of a brotherhood riddled with history, pain, and resentment. Like all brotherhoods, I suppose. I love my brothers. I love that they're here with me on this day. I don't pretend everything is all right, because it's not and never has been and never will be. But I can't control that. I know this.

I can control the smile on my face and the poise in my shoulders, as forced as they might be. Only I know the truth.

"There are many beautiful women in Newport," Eddie observes as he pours us each another round of Macallen. "He just gets to marry one of them."

"I hope I'm not intruding on a bonding moment." Dad staunchly shuffles into our holding quarters, regal in his manner yet tired in his gait. "It's time."

Several deep breaths follow. *I can do this. I'm meant to do this.* Thankfully, I'm wearing navy; no one will see the sweat stains seeping through. I might have a fever.

No matter. It's not about me. It's about us.

Chapter 30
Camilla
2008

She looks beautiful. He looks sad.

Chapter 31
Diana
2008

These festivities are unending. At this rate, I'm burnt out on the glamor of it all. But this is my wedding. I'd always envisioned myself a princess bride, in the way every young girl sees herself as Cinderella. But this, the frosting of jewels and too many fabrics all different shades of white (I'm assured by Mum there is such a thing as shades of white)?

A yacht wedding seems appropriate, a nod to Newport Nautical. The thematic underpinnings of the Windsor actions are not lost on me. Though, they think I'm just a pretty face. Young and doe-eyed, yes, I guess I am. But I have eyes, piercingly blue ones at that—eyes that Charles can drown in, like his own. Or so he says, though he lies to me often. He doesn't think I notice, but I do. I may be naive at times—most times, even—but I'm not blind. He doesn't realize how much I see.

For my seventh birthday, my parents threw me a party with camels. I don't remember where they got the camels, or if I ever knew where in the first place. My wedding doesn't have camels.

There is some poetry in all the pomp, though. *Titanic* is one of my favorite movies. The grandeur of this event (or series of events) matches the publicity of the boat and its maiden voyage, and as we know, its tragic sinking.

"Rose is my doppelgänger." I have always claimed this, though I am blonde and busty. Maybe I am misusing the term.

Even so, Charles pays attention sometimes. On this, our wedding day, he has gifted me the most breathtaking of jewels, fitting of a princess. On top of the red velvet box is a note on his personal stationary:

It's a reimagining of the Heart of the Ocean: a blue, heart-shaped center stone, this one a sapphire, in homage to your mother's birthstone, set in a fitted halo of baguettes, in homage to your love of French paninis. Happy wedding day.
Love, Charles

Even in love he is ruthless.

I enjoy the day, happy as it is and should be. My doubts wane with the moon, now a crescent approaching darkness. I was born under a waxing gibbous. Charles does not care for heavenly bodies.

"We are eighty percent water," I state in fact. "Obviously the moon affects the tides within us." It is one of my more profound observations, as Charles is quick to point out I went to USC.

"Perhaps it is the moon's power that inflicts you and your mood swings." Digs are like sand traps for us: littered on golf courses, and no fun at all to step into or get out of cleanly.

"Your dress is spectacular!" Every bride, I'm told, panders over the choosing of her dress like mothers fawn over their newborns. I just wanted something simple and elegant. I got complicated and flashy. I fit the part, though. A concession among concessions to be a part of the Windsor legacy.

Once, for a wedding when I was a kid, each of my parents bought me a dress to wear. I had to choose. On purpose or not, they made me a symbol of their struggle. I don't even remember what dress I chose. Dad married my stepmom without telling me. I found out from the press. The media seems to play the villain in every one of my stories. Us kids weren't even invited to the reception. We won't have kids at our reception, either.

At least today, my wedding dress is a high point.

I commit to love and cherish my husband in front of the many guests that I don't know today and will probably never know in the future. I don't think Charles liked that I didn't include *obey*.

Camilla is here. I avoid eye contact with her. She looks sad.

We sail past the yacht clubs (plural), in and around the islands. Boats honk and people cheer as we float by. I can only imagine what they're thinking:

What a happy couple!
They are going to have such a good life together!
Those flowers must've cost a fortune!
These people must be richer than the Hiltons!
Look at the size of that boat! The insurance alone . . .
Who wouldn't be happy with all that money?

I find some time, minutes only, to myself at the bow of the boat. It's covered in white roses and accented by those string lights I like so much.

It's a Rose and Jack moment. I consider jumping, if only for a second. My Jack is nowhere in sight. I doubt he'd rescue me. He'd probably claim he'd freeze to death.

Then one of the garcons finds me. I'll never be alone again.

Part Two:
The Marriage

Chapter 32
Charles
2008

And that is that. Here, now, we are. On our honeymoon. What does honey have to do with the moon, anyway?

Our estate sits on the east side of Princeville. Once a golf course, we turned it into more of a compound. It still has a golf course. It's just a little more Windsor. What makes it Windsor? For one thing, there's a saltwater pool on the edge of the property that juts out into the Pacific. It's the only legacy feature of the property that remained following Hurricane Iwa in 1982. Raised off the reef via a rock wall, it withstands the ebbs and flows of the surging tides. The home itself is relatively small compared to the size of the property: about 3,000 square feet of house for a two-acre plot. With an elevated foundation and nearly 100 caissons to support the structure, the home meets hurricane standards. The open floor plan capitalizes on the views, creating that indoor-outdoor vibe that so many new builds integrate. I'm happy to say the style is a far cry from the modern white box that is all the rage these days, though the exterior is white board and batten with a double-pitched roof. We also have laouise windows and louvered doors in the common areas. My favorite part is the floors: polished concrete, they were created by mixing an acid-and-base solution with the concrete to invoke an ocean-y blue-green vibe that matches the exterior surroundings. It's quite magnificent.

And then there's the gardens.

Kauai, the Garden Isle, suits me. It's an inside joke with myself that gardens might describe one of the chosen sites of our family real estate investments. Yes, we're in real estate, generally. But this abode is personal.

I love the green. There's so much of it, like one big canopy. Diana will surely love it. How could she not? The property alone offers so much entertainment, from golf to surfing to snorkeling along the private reef that extends in front of the cove. I have a thing for reefs; they're a separate, private world unto their own. I'm jealous of that. A pure, natural paradise, plus all of the perks of a Windsor residence.

"And the rainbow eucalyptus! The bark is a sight, literally like a rainbow. Some people call them the Dr. Seuss trees." Our plane descends upon the airport as I fill Diana in on some of the local flavor. There's so much to consume, I hope she can process it all!

"That sounds lovely, dear. We will visit Hanalei, yes? I've heard the food truck scene is out of this world."

I'm trying not to judge, really I am. But we're spending our time in paradise, and the first thing she asks me about is food trucks?

"Yes, they are. We can visit if you like. Just be careful around your waistline, you're looking a little chubby."

We all need an accountability partner. She knows I'm just trying to help her stay on track. Otherwise, the collective "we" will never hear the end of it from Mum.

I personally am looking forward to peace and quiet. It'll be all too soon that we must re-engage with our duties and make way to NYC for our first appearance as man and wife.

I can already hear the Wall Street herd yucking it up while we ring the first bell. Something to look forward to.

Chapter 33
Camilla
2008

He's probably touching her; holding her. He should. They are married, after all.

Chapter 34

Diana

2008

When he touches me, my first impulse is to flinch and back away. Is that normal for newlyweds?

He's so excited about these Dr. Seuss trees, but he hasn't commented on my waist-cinching sheath dress that makes me look like a very expensive, jewel-encrusted mermaid. A very *skinny*, very expensive, jewel-encrusted mermaid.

I'm glad the wedding is over. What a stressful event. I can think that now; I wouldn't allow myself before. Before, I willed myself to get through it. It required the efforts of all my brain cells.

"It was a magical day." Mom appreciates the pomp, at least, for what it was.

"I am relieved." Dad never separates logic from levity.

Now, we're on our honeymoon at the royal compound of Princeville. How fitting that it should be called Princeville. We used to visit Maui as kids; Mom always loved Kaanapali. I've never been to Kauai.

From what I've read, there are many secret, semi-private beaches to behold. Maybe I can convince Charles to steal away with me and make love. He thinks I'm delicate, like I caught my Taylor Swift feelings after we met on the Fourth of July. The truth is, he's the delicate one. I pity him.

"And the rainbow eucalyptus! The bark is a sight, literally like a rainbow. Some people call them the Dr. Seuss trees." Our plane descends upon the airport as Charles rants and raves about the floral offerings. We're on our honeymoon. I hope we will do honeymoon things that don't involve children's book authors.

"That sounds lovely, dear. We will visit Hanalei, yes? I've heard the food truck scene is out of this world." And there's a little cove just off the main road that's perfect for skinny dipping. The perfect honeymooning activity.

"Yes, they are. We can visit if you like. Just be careful around your waistline, you're looking a little chubby."

I can't catch a break.

Chapter 35
Charles
2008

New York City is a chaotic mess. It's loud and vulgar and dirty and completely unkempt. I will never understand why it's the epicenter of finance and money and all things American wealth. The Statue of Liberty is pretty, though.

The honeymoon was fine, though I'm not sure why Diana was in such a huff for the last few days. It seemed like it had something to do with the windows being open. One ten-hour flight, and she's sullied by jetlag instead of my poor aptitude as a husband. I don't really think she thinks that. I'm just tired from the trip. Maybe.

Our role here is to ring the morning bell on the New York Stock Exchange floor, an honor in American economics if there ever was one. Generations of Windsors relish this honor; Diana and I are the next.

"She's so beautiful," The Media says.

"She will continue the family legacy," The Firm adds.

Diana has her role. She loves me, I know. She has her moments. But don't we all? The pressure is much to ask of anyone, but she knows what she signed up for. I told her.

I've had my moments.

When I was fourteen, riding my bike towards campus before the first bell, I saw her. A ravishing beauty, smiling, sweet, and full chested. It didn't seem natural at the time, for a girl's chest to be that size. She was seventeen. Her name was Summer.

I'd never seen her before. Barely October, the air was brisk and the sun was just lower than it had been the day before, even as it rose. Her blonde hair swept neatly to one side, she wore a yellow sundress that wrapped her body in all the right places. She looked like an extra in one of those high school movies like "She's All That" or "10 Things I Hate About You." Too pretty to be an extra, yet here we are. She carried her notebooks tightly in front of her. At this point, I didn't know she was so graciously endowed.

"Bobby, hey, wait up!" Summer called in the direction of the starting quarterback. He was standing next to the benches by the parking lot, surrounded by his tight ends and offensive line. Obviously they were an item. It all made sense.

As I rode my wheels towards her, Summer turned left and I saw them. I must've looked a second too long, because before I knew it, my front wheel caught a wedge of uneven sidewalk. I somersaulted over my handlebars and onto the pavement, face down.

She didn't see it happen. Thank God.

I'd like to say my ego was more bruised than my nose. That was not the case. My nose required just short of surgical repairs; the doctor basically rebroke and reset it. I'd never known such throbbing in my young life.

"You're lucky," Dr. Chan would say, "that you avoided surgery. Nose jobs are tricky."

I don't think I'm a vain person, but I don't know what I would've done if it scarred.

And that was the day I became a boob guy.

I'm still a boob guy. Diana meets my needs.

"Stand here, sir. You'll want to look towards that camera there for the presentation and actual ringing." A twenty-something kid in a cheap suit guides me to the platform behind the bell, Diana in tow. We sidestep the crowd of other cheap suits that greets us. Behind the pseudo-balcony that looks like it was stolen from the Acropolis, we stand staunchly erect, as dictated by the protocols of press coverage in The Firm's handbook.

There is, indeed, a handbook. My mother wrote it after her marriage to Dad. She's never shared it with anyone but me, she says. "Too much opportunity for leaks." She means press leaks. "We don't need that kind of publicity."

One of the things I like about Diana is that she takes direction well. Most times. She emulates my movements and stays close, like a good wife should.

She looks regal in her pantsuit and pearl drop earrings, like a princess.

Our piece on the balcony is complete lickety split, before we field questions from the press corps down the hall. They always ask the same questions. It's part of our agreements. No surprises.

Until today.

A renowned journalist somehow made her way into the interview room. Her questions were for Diana. Diana never answers questions. It's protocol.

"Diana, you always look put together. Where do you get your inspiration?"

She won't respond. I'm not worried. She knows she shouldn't respond.

But then, she responds. "I don't coordinate my outfits. They are hand-selected by the best staff in Newport. I owe my looks to their incredible eye for style and design."

Not bad. Mum will be pissed, though.

She didn't follow the rules.

Chapter 36

Camilla

2016

A text thread between Charles and Camilla, late at night

Camilla:

You're pretty amazing at touching me.

Charles:

I want to touch you, all over you and up and down you, and in and out . . .

Camilla:

Oh really?

Charles:

Especially in and out!

Camilla:

That's exactly what I need.

Charles:

Is it?

Camilla:

I know it would breathe new life into me. I can't bear a Tuesday night without you.

Charles:

Oh, is that so?

Camilla:

It's Taco Tuesday. I can't enjoy my tacos without you.

Charles:

I enjoy your pink tacos. I add spice to your life, do I?

Camilla:

Yes, you do. You know I like my salsa with chilis.

Charles:

Then you can relax.

Camilla:

Then I'm full and happy.

Charles:

Ah yes, happy. Then what about me? The tough thing is I need you several times a week.

Camilla:

Oh hunny, so do I. I need you all week. All the time.

Charles:

Oh. God. I'll just live up your dress or something. It would be so much easier!

Camilla:

Oh really? What are you going to turn into, a pair of lace panties?

Charles:

Or, God forbid an IUD. Just my luck!

Camilla:

You are a complete idiot. But, even so, I don't hate the idea. In fact I love it.

Charles:

My luck to be lodged inside of you. I would be a champ and stick it out!

Camilla:

Oh, darling!

Camilla:

Oh, I thought of you so much in Costa Rica.

Charles:

Did you?

Camilla:

It's painful and mean that we couldn't be there together.

Charles:

If you could be here, I think about asking Rosie sometimes.

Camilla:

Why don't you?

Charles:

I'm too scared.

Camilla:

Because I think she's in love with you.

Charles:

Mmmmmm.

Camilla:

She'd do anything you asked.

Charles:

She'd tell all the people.

Camilla:

No, she wouldn't, because she'd be much too scared herself of what you might say to her. I think you've got—I'm afraid it's a terrible thing to say—but I think, you know, those sort of people do feel very strongly about you. You've got such a hold over her.

Charles:

Really?

Camilla:

And you're... I think, as usual, you're underestimating yourself.

Charles:

I don't know. She just might be jealous or something.

Camilla:

Ha, oh, well now, that's a good point. I wonder, I guess she might be.

Charles:

You never know, do you?

Camilla:

No, the little green-eyed monster might be lurking inside her. I just mean, you're so good when people are so flattered to be taken into your world, but I don't know that they'd betray your trust. You know, if they were real friends.

Charles:

Really?

Camilla:

I don't.

Silence.

Camilla:

Did you fall asleep?

Charles:

No, I'm here. Always.

Chapter 37

Diana

2008

I don't know what she wants from me.

She's given me literally no guidelines, no feedback, no direction on what I should do, shouldn't do, or how I should do it. It's like expecting a gymnast to perform a tumbling pass who has never done a cartwheel before.

I am not being set up for success. At the beginning, I thought this an oversight. Maybe the valet forgot to tell me where the spare key is. There must be a reason for the controlled media releases and limited exposure to public life.

The reasons are cow crap dipped in gold.

"I didn't know." A common refrain of mine the last—well, since I met Charles on the Fourth of July. I don't like being the dumb one, the one out of the loop. I was always in the loop. I was a song girl!

Always invited to the best parties (that hasn't changed). Always lauded for my beauty and best-dressed ensembles (also hasn't changed).

Never, ever, criticized for trying to be the best version of myself.

"That scene," what Mum calls it, "borders on catastrophe for this family. We're lucky Wall Street didn't revoke our parking permissions!"

Wall Street loves me. Let's be real. Wall Street thinks me an honest alternative to the stuffy Windsor profile and celebrates my sing-songy, belle-of-the-ball presentation.

Also, there's no parking anywhere in New York City. What permissions could she possibly be talking about?

I hear an earful at our foundation dinner the next night. We're in the Hamptons, the poshest part of Long Island. I couldn't tell you which town or community. It doesn't matter to me. But it's beautiful, coastal cottage chic transplanted from Mount Olympus. A cluster of wealthy enclaves. Shingled windmills. Placid bays. A lighthouse or two. It's like Balboa Peninsula, but old and not as busy.

We're seated next to each other, Charles and I. Finally, an occasion where we're not separated by diplomats and Diplo himself. I just want to spend some quality time with my husband.

"Darling, don't you love the ceviche? It's a Spanish delicacy. The fishermen on the east coast are on another level." Fish talk; so hot. Steamy like scallops in a garlic scampi.

"The citrus is so refreshing. It's a tasty dish, my love." I lick my lips suggestively.

Sometimes it's not what you say, but how you say it.

Our table is not on a stage this time, but still towards the front of an outdoor rotunda accented by flaming lamps and floating tealights. Press presence is heavy; the flashes of their cameras offer more light than the lamps and candles combined.

The orchestra—a twenty-piece one—begins to play "A Song With Windsor Significance." I see the wrinkles in Charles' forehead fold knowingly.

He leans over to me, hand on my thigh and danger in his voice. His mum looks on. "Darling, they're playing our song."

I laugh, angelic in my innocence yet demonic in my spirit. I kiss him gently on the cheek, a peck of shared commissary.

Only too abruptly do my eyes lock with Mum's. Her lips form a perfect horizontal line. Linear, unnatural, even for her and all of her straightness.

"That's enough."

Ok, Mum. Is that really necessary? We're bonding, Charles and me. Finally. After so much distance. After so much spectacle unabated by bad press and too many viral pieces of unflattering content.

And, we're pregnant. A boy; thank God. For some reason, this family is way into boys. It seems old fashioned to me, but I don't question it, like most things in this world. To have a life growing inside of me, part Diana, part Charles, all Newport royalty. United in body and bloodlines.

Even so, at the table, abruptly, he drops my hand. The symbolism does not escape me.

Chapter 38

Charles

2008

Mum is right. We shouldn't be canoodling like this. It's unbecoming and not conducive to a future head of the Windsor Group to be caught laughing at the lyrics of some modern-day folk song.

Diana is less than pleased. As soon as we separate our touch, a scowl lands on her face like a mosquito to its latest victim. The sting carries a certain itch, an inconvenient irritation that spreads quickly when you try to soothe it by scratching. She's irritated by the spectacle. Diana doesn't understand. I thought she did. I was told she did.

"We shouldn't be so obvious." It's true; we shouldn't be. We're married. There's no need for overt displays of our affections, even if they are coy and discreet.

"But we're married. What's wrong with a little romance?" Funny how Diana uses marriage to justify the exact opposite of what propriety dictates. Does she know what family she married into? This shouldn't be a surprise. Mum is a figurehead. There's so much to know, so many rules to follow. It's all in the literal rulebook.

It's happening again; flame and fury overtaking my insides. My hands tremble. I shove them in my pockets. My breath deepens. I swallow to fight it. Why, *why* does this happen to me? My anxiety always shows up at the most inopportune times. Then again, when is the opportune time for an anxiety attack? Even when I'm alone with no one can bear witness to my condition but myself, it's torture. Like an unwelcome party guest who refuses to leave when asked politely.

Thank God there's a lull in the program. I'll excuse myself to the restroom and not come back. It's the polite thing to do.

Camilla understands. She's never made me feel bad about my condition. She gives me the courage to fight it. She helps me question the power I give it. I wish she were here to remind me.

Diana? She knows her way home.

Chapter 39

Camilla

2019

"I realized something." I don't know what took me so long. All the signs were there, in black, white, and all the gray. I'm washing my face as Andrew steps out of the shower. It's a beautiful shower, with the turquoise tile and accents and hardware. I designed it. Obviously.

We've been together a long time, Andrew and I. I didn't make the effort to see it, to believe it. I chose ignorance. Ah, how blissful that was.

Until now.

"I don't know how you feel about me." It's shocking, isn't it? To be married to someone whose feelings about you you don't know. Even worse, you don't know if they exist at all.

"I don't know if I'm important to you." How does that happen? To be so happy—or at least, to believe you are, then realize, without warning, that you never were. That happiness, the happiness you thought you felt, was an illusion. Much like control is. Control is an illusion. There's only how we respond.

Andrew doesn't know how to respond. He's had the upper hand this whole time. And he knew it. He's a bastard for taking advantage of me, and I'm a masochist for allowing it.

I am not weak. I am not belittled, nor do I feel lesser than. I am disappointed in my blind hope. Love may be blind, but those *in* love have better vision. I'm running out of hope. It was misplaced all along.

"I love you, babe." His proclamation borders on earnest—the fake kind. It may be true. I'd like to believe it's true. But that doesn't make it enough. Love is often not enough. There needs to be more to support it. Love in a vacuum is like a candle without a flame. What's the point?

"The frustrating part is not whether or not you have feelings for me, but the fact that I don't know what they are. I'd like to know." I don't know how to be any more clear. Either he loves me, or he loves me not. I just want to know the truth.

"I said I love you. Those are my feelings." I want to know more than that. I want to know whether he thinks of me while he's in the shower, or someone else. I want to know that when he sees a gardenia plant, he's reminded it's my favorite flower. I want to know he feels like the luckiest man in the world to be my husband. I suspect, I fear, that not one of these things is true.

We're having three different conversations. There's the one aloud, the one in my head, and the one in his. This isn't going to end well, whatever *this* is—parallel conversations that never meet. In so many ways the same, but never intersecting.

He's not going to tell me. He's not vulnerable like that, not how Charles is. It's one of Charles' best qualities. Andrew would be irresistible if he had even a shred of vulnerability.

He does not. And I cannot change him.

"I'm not starting a fight. I'm expressing myself." I stand firm in my stance, redundant as it may be.

"I don't understand what you're trying to express." He furrows his brow and crosses his arms over his chest. His pectorals are so busty they compress with the gesture. "I told you I love you. And you love me. Isn't that enough?"

It's never enough. I've always known this. Maybe not *always*, but certainly as an adult, following years of commingling with men, I learned love is not just about the emotion itself, but the actions that show love and support the emotion. The tangible acts that support intangible feelings. That's what makes love. The absence is what breaks it.

"No, Andrew. It's not." Could I have been more direct and succinct in communicating my discontents? Maybe. Could Andrew have been more interested in understanding my point of view? Clearly.

The fact is, we weren't. And the only way out is forward.

"I want a divorce."

Chapter 40

Diana

2012

He just . . . left me. No explanation. I didn't even know he left the event until the car arrived at the valet.

He's a connoisseur of the Irish goodbye. And he's not even Irish, as far as I know.

When I get home, I tear off my suffocating straitjacket of a ballgown. I wore my nice lingerie tonight with the idea that maybe we could have a night of pleasure. Maybe something laced by touching and teasing. Our fire feels like a cooling ember these days. It makes me sick.

I never thought I'd want to throw up food that tasted so good on the way into my body. Something to be savored. Eating can be its own act of pleasure, especially when coated in French chocolate or bathed in a lemon butter sauce.

I throw up because it gives me control. I control what goes in, I control what comes out. It gives me power. It gives me assurance I have some sense of control over my life and how I spend my hours. Charles comments on my threadbare appearance as if in disgust.

"Baby, darling, those clothes don't hang right on you. Maybe ease off on the cheese rolls. Porto's gets enough business from the Mexicans and Asians."

There is so much wrong with this commentary, I don't even know where to begin. I may be from Newport, but I also know a thing or two about human decency. Sometimes I wonder if Mum forgot to instill those values in her precious heir, as diabolically inconsistent as he is.

How hard is it to understand that I have feelings? That his actions affect my feelings? Sometimes I wonder if he even has them himself. I am at a disadvantage. I've never had a serious boyfriend before, let alone a relationship steeped in the most concentrated toxicity of modern family dynamics. It's dopey. It's cruel. It's unrelenting.

"Now, Miss D, don't cry." Claudia makes solemn attempts at soothing me. She has been a godsend, though I'm still not sure if she's someone I can trust. "He's just a man. Men love bitches."

"Bitches?" *Why would men love bitches?*

I learn Claudia is a devout follower of the self-help book of the same name. "It changed my life. Men love me. They don't feel trapped by me. In fact, they appreciate that I don't have feelings, or appear to have feelings. That is the difference."

Appear to have feelings? I'm intrigued by the thought, but there's no chance I'm capable of it—hiding my feelings inside, within, like a secret inaccessible even to the most worthy. Or those who *should be* the most worthy. Like, say, a husband. I swear it's part of the definition of a husband. Someone to confide in, someone to share pains with, someone to endure with, to coexist with. Is this such a fantasy? Am I living in an alternate reality?

I guess, in the beginning, I sort of hid myself. I showed him a version of me I thought he wanted. Now, I just want him to want me for me.

What is this bitch business? I don't know how to be a bitch. I don't even know how to be a bad girl. Perhaps, even more deeply, I don't know how to be a wife. Maybe I just don't know how to be Charles' wife. How's that for introspection, Camilla?

I threw myself down the stairs after we fought last night. I am a physical target for my own pain. No broken bones, at least. I'm suffering, obviously. It didn't occur to me that I could lose my child, or injure him at the very least. Or, maybe it did, but the thought didn't stick. It's fleeting, like every other thought and feeling I have these days. Living in my thoughts is almost as bad as living in the Windsor World: wracked with rules, regulations, and really weird definitions of respect.

My own existence is wrapped in the disappointment of my father, who wanted a son so badly but then got me. I wasn't even named until a week after I was born. Then reality set in. At least he eventually got my brother. My son will never experience this, thank God. I honestly don't know if Dad ever respected me, not really. All because I wasn't a boy. How could I control that?

The Windsor family doesn't respect me. I just want to be loved. I want the love my parents never had. Maybe that's silly? It's not like Liz and Phil (they hate that I call them that) are the best examples of a happy, modern marriage. Maybe we were doomed from the start, Charles and me. Our relationship models are empty of any happiness, of any true love. Dad and Mom suffered each other. They didn't love each other. Maybe we can break the cycle. Maybe. As long as we don't break each other's' necks first.

We had a date night, finally, just the two of us, not including Pablo loitering in the bar behind the main dining room, called Sidedoor. I like this restaurant, the Five Crowns. It's an old English inn, complete with a red telephone booth outside. There's a greenhouse off the back that looks like a fairies' paradise. It's light and airy. Otherwise the space is dark, marked by the history of old mahogany. The contrast is paradoxically beautiful. The wine captain has worked here since the seventies. He's British, too.

It's a kind irony, a tribute to the sense of place that's often overlooked. Sometimes it's hard to get past the shiny stuff. Sometimes, the shiny stuff is all there is: waterford crystal stemware accented with diamonds. Silk born of silkworms from the most exclusive region of China. A G Wagon license plate that reads B FLEXIN. What then? Go back to the times when life was simple and living was easy. What is easy? What is right? Expectation kills dreams. Just ask Charles.

Tonight is the ballet. I have a special treat planned for Charles. I know he enjoys "Uptown Girl." Who doesn't love a good Billy Joel performance? I hope he'll be proud. I've been working so hard to perfect my pirouettes. I've always loved ballet, though I'm too tall to have ever been considered a serious candidate for a principal dancer in any worthy company.

Last year we did a number together. That was before. Now, I want to honor him on my own, with my own demonstration of skill and grace. And skinniness. You can see my ribs through my leotard. He damn well better be proud. I'm doing this all for him.

From the stage, we make eye contact. There's a storm behind those eyes; I can see it clearly, even with the stage lights shining blindly in my face. I wish I was blind right now.

I can only imagine what he's thinking. My suspicions will later be confirmed:

Undignified.
Too thin.
Too showy.

So much for my attempt at showing my love.

Chapter 41
Charles
2012

I'm tailspun, if that's even a word. I am spinning, round and round, out of control. Not even the coastguard can save me from this misery, from this ill-advised world of rules and relationships gone rogue.

What was she thinking, to flaunt herself like that? She knows I despise it when she shows off like that. The attention whore. Apparently she didn't get enough of it in college, when all those frat boys couldn't lift their gazes from her nipples. I don't blame them. But she's a married woman now. She should know how to prevent such provocative behavior. It's her body.

"I did it for you, my love." I notice the red blood vessels webbed in her eyes, like gold veins in Calcutta marble. She doesn't know what love means.

I treat her with silence the rest of the night. She looks like an abandoned puppy, begging me for scraps of food and recognition. And belly rubs. She gets none of the above. She gets a frosty shoulder. She gets a ride home. She doesn't get validation. She's looking in the wrong place for that.

I fell off a boat today. It was bound to happen. Camilla says I'm not very seaworthy. She's right, per usual.

"Do you admit when you're wrong?" I'm curious.

"I'm trying to think of the last time I was wrong." At least Camilla is honest. Telling.

Diana fumes at me. Suddenly she's found her voice. Perhaps it was lost, and now she's found.

How convenient, the timing.

I have this idea, a PR stunt, one that would send the press down a spiral of stopwatches and bunny rabbits, ending with a castigation by the Queen of Hearts.

Hear me out. My arm is broken. During my press conference announcing my recovery, I reveal a FAKE ARM. Ha! It's brilliant. That will put those vultures in their place.

I mention it to Diana, not that I need her approval or support, but I'm curious what she thinks. She gives me a scalp massage and I forget about it pretty fast.

Coincidentally, the arm disappears the next day. Must've been mistaken as a prop for a theatre show or something. Oh, well. Yet another missed opportunity.

Birth Announcement: William Windsor

2008

Diana Spencer Windsor was safely delivered of a son at 6:09 a.m. today. Madame Windsor and her child are both doing well.

Chapter 42

Camilla

2013

I wanted to share my feelings. Not thoughts. Feelings. My thoughts and feelings often coexist; sometimes it's uncomfortable, sometimes it's pure misery. Most times, it's a deep cut healing itself, not without the searing fire of sowing skin. Like dried blood, scabbed yet wet with red.

My monologue begins.

"I feel like I'm standing outside a glass house." He looks at me with the eyes that acknowledge my propensity for metaphors and his secret pride in them. "I'm here, on the threshold, looking in. I can see what's going on inside, I see it all. I see you, flitting about as you do when preparing for guests. But I can't hear anything. It's a silent film of homemade hospitality. A story is unfolding, but I only have access to part of it.

"I ring the doorbell. While I wait, in my hands I hold my housewarming gift: an armful of love."

Love. He shivers. He doesn't expect this from me, the tough cookie. No matter how tough the cookie, the main ingredient is still always sugar. I'm sweet most days. He hasn't seen this yet, the soft, chewy center of a Bordeaux bar. On most days, I'm a chip of molasses. To him, at least. It's just because I don't pity him. Now, he gets to see.

"I'm standing here, with all this love to give, while I wait for you to answer the door. Sometimes, yes, it takes a few minutes to answer the door. You might be in the bathroom or flipping a skillet over the stove. Even though I know you don't cook."

He smiles then, knowingly, without knowing what's coming next.

"Other times, it's faster because everything is set and ready for entertainment. While I wait outside, on the threshold with potted petunias and coleus, the load of love I'm carrying is getting heavier." I gesture my hands in the shape of a box in front of my body, to indicate the physical existence of this idea. Something concrete. Something with shape. "You know how even the lightest object can feel heavier over time? That's how my love feels. With every passing moment, my love becomes heavier, becomes increasingly more difficult to hold up, while I wait for you to answer the door."

His demeanor is now solemn, his head bent forward as if in prayer. I know he's listening.

"I could throw a rock at the glass house, but what good would that do? It's probably bulletproof. Entry by force is not my thing. That's not how I want to get inside. I want to be invited in.

"Eventually, the weight of my love will be too much for me to bear. If no one answers the door, I have to assume no one is home, even if I can see through the glass. I have to assume the home is not ready for a housewarming. The home is not ready for my love.

"And so, in the end, I'll walk away and take my love with me. And that will be that. I don't say this in contrast to your own needs to find yourself before you find yourself with me. I say this in parallel, in coexistence with everything you feel. I feel too. And while I admire your conviction, my feelings are my feelings. My thoughts are my thoughts. And I thought you should know where I stand, sit, and stay.

"But let's be clear. I'm not your chocolate lab. I'm a Siberian husky, loyal yet fiercely independent."

It's time to breathe, now. I'm not naturally good with silence. I'm more comfortable with chaos. But sometimes, silence is necessary.

"How much longer until your arms give out?" I appreciate his participation in my metaphor, no matter how perfunctory his line.

"I work out, so you have a few minutes before these limbs need a break."

Without missing a beat, he smiles coyly. "Next time, I'll leave you a key under the mat."

Chapter 43

Diana

2010

Top of the World—a local hiking trail and park in Laguna Beach, California

Breathtaking.

Both the views, and Charles' obnoxious claims of being the global authority on climate change.

"You see how the wildflowers are dry and ashen? They're parched."

He speaks to me as though I have no baseline knowledge to speak of. I'm a broken record now. I went to USC! While it might not be the hallowed halls of Stanford, or even the bastard Bruins of UCLA (I'm obligated to say that), Charles refuses to consider my mind as one consisting of thought, of worthy contributions to conversation.

"What about the homelessness situation, darling? I've heard such awful reports from the city council. What do you think should be done?" He's belittled my interest in the topic before. So I bring it up again.

His empty glare hangs palpably between us and the sweet smell of California poppies, newly bloomed on the hillsides. Canyons and coastline stretch near and far as we stand at the epicenter of height and length.

"That is a very complicated problem, Diana. I don't know that you have the mental capacity to understand such things." He guzzles endlessly from his Hydro Flask before stopping mid-gulp to accuse me of watching Channel 3 instead of preparing for my next media blitz.

I can't decide if he's gaslighting me, or if he's really just an insecure man with too much power.

I go back and forth. Regardless of the truth, the fact is: he's an asshole.

I love him anyway.

Besides, what else is there, if there isn't love?

I'm disappearing, slowly but surely. In this most physical and existential ways. I bet he doesn't even think I know what "existential" means. He's never noticed my mind. Or the scars left by the blades of the lemon slicer on my thighs.

My patience is flimsy these days, like the stilts I have for legs. I'm a newborn fawn learning the definition of upright. The execution needs work. I share this trait with my child, William. His smile lights up my life. "Mother" is the most important title I'll ever have.

"Where are you going?" Charles calls to me as I descend the trail towards the ocean.

When words fail, action always seems to get his attention.

I may be young. I may be beautiful. I may, at times, be a bit naive. But I am not stupid.

I continue a few paces before digging my Nike-clad foot into the brush and about-facing towards the man who bears the title of "husband," but seems to prefer behaving like a childish goat.

"Why do you speak to me like that?"

"Like what?"

"With such contempt?" I wait. The membrane that coats his thick head sometimes needs a moment or two for information to seep into the brain cells. If it does at all.

Charles stands above me, on the incline of soil that moistens the earth and captures the little rainwater we've had in the last ten years of drought. In a way, he always stands above me. He is the chieftain, and I—I am the ruled.

At least we have a son. I love my son. I don't love how the press invades our privacy, how the Firm demands so much of my time, but won't support mother-son bonding time. I had to fight with the jaws of life for them to allow him to join us on a tour *days* after he was born. I've never cried or fought so hard. Charles fought, too, but more with me than on my behalf. Patterns.

His brow furrows like a caterpillar inching along a bed of needles. "You think I speak to you with contempt?"

"I *know* you speak to me with contempt." I pause, considering whether to continue with the fatal blow, a potential point of no return. Aren't we already there? I proceed. "You never speak to Camilla this way."

Camilla. His kryptonite.

"Camilla stands on her own, without cause for contempt. You, you waddle along, course-corrected by staff and not-staff, to make sure you don't waver into the land of the unforgivable."

"Unforgivable? What you're doing, my dear Charles, is unforgivable."

"And what is that?"

"Adultery."

I wait some more. I hope he'd be surprised by my audacity. I think that's what it's called. Balls.

"It's not adultery when you care for the person."

I didn't see that one coming, as sharp as my 20-20 vision might be. But then again, I couldn't have seen this spontaneous combustion from my balconied suite, let alone the stratosphere.

"What is it, then? I'm dying to know." Am I, though?

"It's called love."

He does this to hurt me, to carve out any remaining seeds of soul that may have once been planted for him. Like a love fern. These are more like love spores, toxic and terribly useless.

"I think this lecture is over." My attempt at strength is somewhat convincing. "I'd like to go home."

"You know the way."

Princely in posterity, while impoverishly devoid of propriety. At least when it comes to me.

He would never send Camilla home like this. He loves her, after all.

What if I disappeared? Ended it all? I doubt anyone would miss me.

"Whatever happens, I'll always love you."

I don't know what else I expected to hear. It's my own fault, hiding behind the door to his office, hoping, praying, it would go another way.

I'm immature and don't handle such things well. So I yelled and screamed and broke a few things. I threw a baby bottle at the chandelier in his office. The dangling prisms reacted to the earthquake of what's probably a combination of my raging hormones and raging hate.

His response to my tantrum? "You're overreacting."

Overreacting? You're oversimplifying the problem, DEAR.

I have my own secrets.

His eyes, they spear me like wicked tuna caught off the shores of Catalina. I sense his posture relax when we're alone. Which is not often. But often enough for words to evolve into phrases that make sentences of witty banter between lovers.

You see me.
I see you.
Where does your heart lay?
In my bad dreams.

Sleepless, shapeless
Nights that creep tasteless
into our lives
sultry and chasteless.
Speak to me, you dark angel,
cunning and faceless.

A spirit that hovers, lurks
haunting, harrowed, weightless,
screams silent, no fear,
punctuated by a braised kiss,
Sing to me, you tempt'uous devil,
beguiling and fateless.

Dreams, may they come,
swiftly and angstless
into our sleeps,

soulful and sanctless.
Pray for me, you hopeful human,
may your armored heart be gateless.

He's married, you know. Since when does a contract like that forbid truancy?

It doesn't. Just ask Charles.

"I love guarding your body."

He's punny, this one. I love a good pun, even if I don't understand them. I appreciate the attempt. It shows an agility of the mind.

"Guard me like a pot of gold."

"You are my rainbow." Barry isn't afraid of me.

I wonder if he speaks to his wife this way.

Not like it matters.

He gives me hope. After I've thrown up all of it.

Derelict. I'm not sure what that means. Charles has accused me of being it after I got home late one night. Late, because I broke curfew like some rebellious teenager. I feel like I'm a rebellious teenager, more often than not.

I should look it up. But most of me doesn't care. So I won't.

He held me, Barry did, like letting go was the worst thing in the world. Tangled in skin, we dance in the sheets like ribbons winding around a maypole, only sexier. I forgot what it's like to be touched with angsty desire, like that rebellious teenager defying Daddy's dating rules. We had it right, back then. Pure passion for passion's sake, no complication of sex. Sex is good when it's good, when you're in love.

Maybe I love too easy.

I'd rather that than not at all. Sometimes pleasure and pain are one and the same.

Chapter 44

Charles

2015

"She deserves to know."

My skin tingles at the thought of the world finding out about our secret—again. I don't feel guilty. Still, though, I am involved, if only in the orbit of an institution I was born into and cannot escape. It's the Firm, and all its bylaws that tether me to it.

My index finger circles the rim of my neat whiskey. The somber ambiance of Bosscat matches the tone of our dialogue. There are bottles of the stuff everywhere. It reminds me of what a speakeasy would have looked like during prohibition. Most of the people here are passing through town; John Wayne Airport is just down the street. Unlikely anyone would recognize us, except Gabe, the bartender. We sit in a booth across from the hightop bar that hosts the financiers and fickle fast-talkers of the local scene. Our conversation holds a different air, one of angst and sadness.

Petra knows. She has generally known, privy to the Firm's innerworkings. She looks across the mahogany table top and into my sorry excuse for pupils. Even when dilated, they shrink away from the light.

"What problem would that solve?" Everyone loves the catfight narrative. I have some ideas. Problems are relative, as are solutions. I'm not sure if solutions exist. Temporary fixes? Maybe. Everything is temporary. Including and especially love.

"Her unhappiness," she states matter-of-factly. "And your guilt." In a gesture of decision, she washes these away with a sip of chardonnay, a Santa Barbara varietal, I think.

Guilt. What a powerful motivator that is.

I have guilt. I am only human. After all, all the wealth in the world cannot insulate one from pain. It can make it more bearable, I guess. But also more empty. More lonely. There are fewer people who can empathize. That is one of Diana's strengths: her empathy. I've never seen so much compassion. I would never tell her that, though. How would that make me look?

Weak.

I've tried to help her in all her bouts of depression. I even called my mentor, the Professor, to read her poetry and soothe her.

She just sulked, as she does. I'm only trying to make her happy. I'm trying the only way I know how. It's exhausting when all she does is pout. She's such a child sometimes. We already have one, with another on the way. She needs to grow up.

"You're being selfish." I claim this not to deflect my own internal qualms. Petra is, in absolute terms, acting selfish.

"Maybe. I'd rather be selfish than selfless in this scenario." She has never been one to bury her burdens. The Firm doesn't know that.

Petra finishes her glass before whispering her parting words. "If you don't tell her, I will."

At least she gives me that courtesy. Sometimes she acts like she doesn't even work for the Firm, or the Family. That's what makes her a good press manager. She stands, slides her Gucci clutch under her left arm, and struts away. The clack of her heels echoes before fading on the other side of the room.

I'm left alone, a mix of paltry and provoked.

It's mounting, the build-up. All too familiar and all too franken. My breath quickens. My heat, it beats, thumps, paces, like Queen's *We Are the Champions*.

I'm not a champion. I'm not a winner. I'm a pawn. I don't own my choices.

I want for nothing. I have it all. Yet, I have none of it. The Firm, the fiction, rules us all. This intangible entity lays claim to the choices we make. Who's "we"? Mum? Even she lives at the mercy of this corporate law. We're a family. We're a firm. It's a battle distinguishing the two. Even the idea of a family business oversimplifies the heart of how it operates: with strength, but also with struggle.

I struggle for air, for breath, for life. This is an internal battle, between my ears and behind my eyes. No one else can see it. They see the side effects; perhaps the sweat over my brows or the subtle tremble in my carpals. But they don't see the pain. That is another level of consciousness. Most will never know it. I envy them and their ignorance.

Such bliss I will never know.

I leave a one-hundred-dollar bill to cover the tab. I'm halfway to the exit when my phone buzzes.

It's her.

A wave of calm collides with my pathetic excuse for a coastline, ripped and rippled, ugly.

"Hi." I answer as evenly as I can manage.

"What's wrong?" She knows me so well.

"Milla, my love. I don't know what to do."

Chapter 45

Camilla

2015

"Tell me everything." He's lucid, that much I can infer from his delicate tone. He's probably having an episode.

He spills, pours himself to me, like an overflowing river after a downpour. At times I can't make sense of the words. I let him go on. No sense in interrupting. I get the gist just fine.

When he finishes, his silence begs me for answers. I have no answers. Only empathy. Compassion.

It's not my job to fill him up; only he can do that. But I can listen and support him, even when I'm involved in less-than-flattering ways. It's one of my strengths.

"Wow." My awe is genuine. "That sounds like a tough situation. What are you going to do next?" I ask a lot of questions, like a therapist might. You can bring a horse to water but you can't make it drink, even if it's really thirsty.

Charles is a strong man, even if he refuses to believe it or act like it. It's entirely possible to be both strong and insecure. It's a tenuous distinction sometimes. He can bury his feelings in strength like the best of them. He's a leader in that way.

But sometimes, his insecurity gets the better of him. He runs away, hiding, like a house mouse into his hole in the wall.

"Nothing."

Of course. "Sounds like avoidance to me."

"So?"

"You are brave. I've shared this with you before. Do you think avoidance is the answer?"

His breath lengthens. A sigh follows a chortle. "I much prefer to hide than to fly. It's more private that way."

"Maybe there's another way."

"What way?"

"Letting go."

"How?"

"Vulnerability."

"I am vulnerable."

"Crying doesn't make you vulnerable. It can be an outburst of emotion, a reaction when someone isn't able to manage their emotions."

"Are you saying I don't know how to manage my emotions?"

"Yes." It's time to be direct. "You avoid them. You don't manage them." I pause. "Maybe it's time to rethink that approach."

"I don't know how."

I know. I always suspected. Now what?

Birth Announcement: Harry Windsor

2011

Diana Spencer Windsor was safely delivered of a son at 8:48 p.m. today. Madame Windsor and her child are both doing well.

Chapter 46
Diana
2013

"Welcome aboard, my lady." James wears his skipper's hat well, nestled atop a head of thick, curly brown hair. His locks are tucked neatly beneath the brim, peaking out slightly. He doesn't look like an adulterer, but then again, neither do I. I don't think.

"Might I come aboard?" He takes my hand as I step up onto the deck of the *Porterhouse*, anchored at the mooring just across from the bay club where eyes wander like the vagabonds they are. It can never be easy.

At least the night protects us. The lights around the bay are magical. I'm a sucker for mood lighting, and the flicker of sidelights and anchor lights puts me in the mood.

James has been teaching me how to sail. I'm not as good as Camilla, but I am learning. James says I have talent, and I choose to believe him.

"Pappy Van Winkle for you?" He knows me. There's something about the burn of bourbon. Neat, always neat. No need to dilute its power.

"Thank you, my love." I have a bad habit of falling in love. James treats me like the princess I am and deserve to be. I might not be royalty, but I am worthy.

I take the lowball glass from James and sip my poison. Our time together is so . . . peaceful. Like the sea without wind. It gives me hope while also bringing a sadness.

I'm tired today. Charles yelled at me some more about a bad interview I gave to the media about another hospital opening.

"I don't understand why you can't keep to the cue cards. Any literate moron could do that. Why can't you?" And then I threw up the shrimp cocktail I ate for lunch.

James cooks for me. He's a working stay-at-home dad, manning his vessel and taking care of his woman. I like that.

"How about panko-crusted salmon over rice with a side of arugula and ponzu sauce?" He sears his salmon on the stove. It turns pink like strawberry Starburst. Wild rice simmers while James tosses his arugula in a deep bowl. He throws out the most wilting pieces.

"I love it when you talk dirty."

We eat on cocktail stools by candlelight consisting of two white tapers held by sterling silver. We chide and laugh and steal food from each other's plates. It's magically simple, being here with him.

We punctuate our dinner with a glass of port. I've never been fancy like that, but I enjoy the ritual we've created here: our own, and no one else's.

"Do you like the new bedding I got for the captain's quarters?" James leads me with his eyes to the suite where we sleep on the nights when I can get away. At least I know how to operate the Boston Whaler. James taught me.

The duvet is a creamy white with delicate points of gathered fabric, mimicking the ocean. Oversized pillows accent the headboard, upholstered with matching colors. Threaded with navy blue stitching, the sleeping place is like a nautical cloud of paradise.

"Cozy, honey." I slide my backside along the foot of the bed. I lay back, inviting James to take me away. "Sleepy?" I smile coyly.

"Not even a little."

We make love like it's going out to style. He kisses me in all the right places. He knows where my tender spots are. He's gentle and kind, like Venus in Gemini. As the sunrise peaks over the hills of Newport Coast, I'm docking the whaler and walking up the landing to my entrance in the back of the bayside compound. No one sees me.

Chapter 47

Charles

2013

Refugio State Beach, Goleta, California—morning

"Do you mind if I take my clothes off?"

She obviously knows the answer. What warm-blooded man would respond with anything but the affirmative?

We're completely alone, hidden away from onlookers down the stretch of beach that most people are too lazy to walk towards. She could've chosen one of the limestone caves to disrobe in. Concaved in the hillside, it's the perfect place for some sexual shenanigans. But that's just not Milla's style.

Maybe it was, once upon a time. When she was young, and proper, and maybe a little scared of living. Today, though, she's a blazing comet that lights up my darkest nights. And, if I'm being honest, my days, too.

"Don't let me stop you." I lay in the sand while she takes off her oversized cardigan. She throws it down like a beach towel next to me and our eyes meet in a tango of torture. What is love, if not torture? This secrecy gives me anxiety, but she's worth it.

One Beach Boys band tee and pair of joggers later, she's sunning her already-bronzed body next to mine. I look like powdered sugar compared to her. I prop myself up on my left elbow and turn towards her, protecting her from any spectators who might otherwise want to witness our soft porno. My hand grazes her breasts. I know she won't object.

"That feels nice." She confirms my suspicion. "I love your big hands."

And we kiss, long and lustful, under a brightly brimming sun. No one exists but us, and the colony of birds pecking at sand crabs along the waterline. I wish that we could hide here forever, away from the chaos that is real life.

"You're the only person I would do this with." I tease her gently, rubbing her between her legs. The small of her back lifts up, reacting to my fingers. I slide my free hand under her, wrapping around her like a swaddle might.

"Likewise." She gasps, her voice raspy with want. The heat of our bodies combined with the sun burns into our skin. This scene really is romantic: the waves, the wind, the juju that is buried in these beaches.

I never thought I'd deserve this kind of love. I never saw my dad touch my mom. Theirs was a marriage of manners, uniting two great families to create one really large real estate empire.

On our way back to the car, we look for sand dollars and fossils. Camilla likes driftwood, too. "The texture reminds me of the waves, timeless and unending." She's deep sometimes, a lot of times, actually. I like that about her.

We have until tomorrow before we return to our respective realities. Me, to my buildings, to my wife. She, to her clients, to her husband.

Everything ends. At least we have the night. At least we have each other. Even if just for now.

Chapter 48

Camilla

2013

Emerald Cove, Laguna Beach, California—evening

His open mouth consumes me. I warned him. "I'm completely bare under here." I point to my white shift dress. It's flowy and hides my curves. He doesn't care. Before I know it I'm straddling him, completely naked, completely free. He touches me delicately, with a firmness reserved for desire. He removes his shirt overhead so we're skin on skin above our hips. I breathe into his neck. He rubs the length of my back, upward towards my neck, and kisses me.

"You are something else." Aren't I, though? I was never ordinary, too pretty to be smart and too smart to know how to use it. I'm thirty-two now, and embracing my wholeness. My water and my fire.

I didn't expect to be an adulteress. It's not one of the things you aspire to be when you're a kid. A successful businesswoman; a high-ranking official; a good person. Never an adulteress. But what do you do when you love someone outside of your marriage? Love doesn't discriminate. Shakespeare said love is blind. Isn't that the truth.

What do you do when you love someone outside of your marriage? Accept the label. In naming, we give the thing we are naming power. I am an adulteress to those who view our love as shameful, as an act of infidelity betraying the institution of marriage. Love and marriage are not one and the same, nor are they mutually exclusive. I used to think that was the case. I don't anymore. Our affairs, they are an evergreen accusation that straddles truth and . . . whatever the opposite of truth is. A lie? Sometimes, truth is an act of rebellion. Sometimes, we show up as ourselves and others can't handle it because it's not consistent with the truths that they hold or learned or came to believe. Truth is personal.

"You see me," Charles confides in me as we spoon in the overly luxurious king-sized bed with views of the Pacific Ocean. Tonight, the moon is a waxing gibbous—not quite full, but full of light. The silhouettes of palm trees and tide pools below shine in the darkness, like igneous rock formed way past the time of flowing lava.

"But it's so dark! Only the night can see us now." I speak in poetry. This night is a poem, a tribute to what we are and what we can never be: two flawed people who weren't supposed to fall in love.

"Just the way I like it."

Chapter 49

Diana

2013

"Diana, I have something to tell you," Charles rasps through the closed door to my suite.

We're sleeping separately now; it suits both of our lifestyles. He hardly ever makes a personal appearance. He usually sends Rupert.

"What, Charles?" I don't try to hide my contempt. Our point of no return has long since eclipsed.

He pushes the door ajar and finds his way across the threshold. I'm fixed on some correspondence to one of the charity leagues with whom I'm obligated to maintain relations. Despite our disunity, we are still legally tethered to each other, and I for one will not be the one to burn any metaphorical bridges.

At least, not yet. I will on my own terms.

"Barry is dead."

His emotional capacity is that of a brick wall. How does someone process a delivery like that? I would have preferred a courier pigeon to this pathetic excuse for a personal touch.

I stare at him, empty of soul. "What?" is all I can say.

"He was killed in a motorcycle accident. I'm very sorry."

Murderer is my first thought. Reactionary, yes, but not completely unfounded. He would do anything to spite me. He knows no bounds. His extramarital relationship is more than enough proof, as far as I'm concerned.

Even at my blondest, my skinniest, arguably my most desirable in the eyes of the Newport Nautical crowd, I am not enough. I'm not even enough to be left alone to enjoy my own life within this pathetic excuse for a family business. It's not a family business. It's a monstrous turpentine of a system designed to monopolize power and control, and the people are its servants, its enforcers. It's brilliant, yet utterly inhuman.

I yell and scream, cry and suck air like I'm drowning beyond the shore break. Charles stands there and watches. I'd like to think he's protecting me from myself, but I don't think that's true. I think he's protecting me from himself, from his future, from any bad press. It's selfish, but what else is there?

"Are you done yet?" After a few minutes of silence passes, he leaves me to my grief. And my next binge begins.

I can pretend to be surprised. But what good would that do? It's clear to me the Firm and the Family are not my advocates, no. They are my adversaries.

Where does Charles fit in all of this? Where does he fit in the lives of our children?

Divorce. I never thought I would divorce. I am young.

I am also bulimic and unhappy. Which is worse?

We've been walking around this exhibition on Vancouver Island for four hours. No food. I haven't eaten for days. Control. When I say that, I mean food staying down. We're walking around and around, dizzy with all the responsibility that comes with this life. I can't tell anyone my body is betraying me. They'll just think I'm making excuses or something unsupportive and vindictive.

I miss my boys. My sources of unending, and only joy.

Then it happens.

"Darling, I feel like I am disappearing." I've evaporated, like a puddle after a rainstorm during a drought. Unexpected and not supposed to exist in the first place.

He leaves with me, accompanies me to the hospital, and ensures the right people are notified of my admission. I give him credit for that.

"Why couldn't you have just waited until later to cause a scene?"

I. Just. Can't. Anymore.

A fancy event or your wife's health. Who knew there was actually a choice to be made? I'd choose him every time. It's clear he wouldn't do the same. If I had to bet on it, he would always choose Camilla, even if she wasn't one of the choices. He'd make sure she was one of the choices.

I've lost myself. I don't recognize me anymore, the bones peeking through a layer of skin so tanned with orange spray; my blonde hair so platinum it rivals (someone with really blonde hair). My eyes so sunken they resemble capsized diamonds, levitating in salt water. I'm not even sure diamonds float in salt water. Or at all.

"Better yet, you could have passed out behind a door. That would have been better."

I don't know anything about fainting. How could I? It's my first time.

Charles isn't having it. Even at my bedside, his lips are taut and devoid of comfort. His handsome facade is such a tease. Word to the wise: book covers are marketing content; it's only when you start reading that you have a sense of what the story is really about.

"You must pull it together, Di. We have dinner with one of our most important clients tonight." He's serious. I am riddled with pain, and his concern is hobnobbing with the Wrights.

"But darling," I plead, "I am desperate for rest. I am very weak." He must see it. It's written all over my gauntly feeble face.

"You must go out tonight. Otherwise everyone will think there is something awfully wrong. I don't need the drama."

Because everything is always about him and how it looks. What about how it feels?

Chapter 50

Charles

2013

"My wife is feeling much better now than she was earlier in the afternoon. And it's entirely due to the extremely advantageous conditions that pertain in British Columbia—the weather and the general fertile conditions—which have ensured she's about to have sextuplets, which is really why she fainted."

No one is laughing. "It's actually not true."

Tough crowd.

I thought it was funny.

Diana; always stealing the spotlight. Even when she's not here!

It pisses me off, all of it—that she's so good at the job. That all anyone wants is to shake her hand or take her picture. Never in my tenure have I been embraced with such love.

She hasn't earned it. I've invested so much time and energy, and my ROI is nil. Sometimes I think I was born into the wrong body. Maybe God made a mistake.

Even so, here I am. I am me. Making speeches and shaking hands with the top one percent and their political counterparts. They might as well be one and the same. Power runs with power.

Which is ironic. Most times, I feel powerless.

I felt powerless as a kid, too. Threatened with military school, even when I didn't do anything to prompt discipline. Except that one time when I set that neighbor's cat on fire. He deserved it. It would terrorize my lab constantly.

In some ways, you could say I lived in fear. Fear of abandonment. Fear of rejection. All because I simply existed as myself. Sometimes I catch myself overexplaining why I do things. Like explaining will decrease the likelihood of this abandonment, of this rejection. Like it's insurance against these things happening to me. Like I can control the outcome. Or at least, my brain thinks I can control the outcome.

That's all that matters. Our life is what our thoughts make it. Or at least how we can or can't control them.

Chapter 51

Camilla

2015

"Okay, boys, I'm just going to have a quick word with Camilla and I'll be up in a minute."

This woman has no sense. On my sister's birthday, no less, she decides to stage an insurrection and all but corner me. Someone send help.

Charles and his buddy look at each other before obliging Diana's request. His buddy leaves first, practically skipping up the stairs posthaste. Charles looks at me. I nod, acknowledging the imminent reality that Diana and I will be alone, without chaperones.

I understand her pain, though. It doesn't feel good. It doesn't feel like anything, really. Mostly numbness, with a spear of betrayal the size of a nuclear warhead. Maybe more intense.

I've heard whispers of her eating issues. Charles whispers to me. His voice has a depth I've never known, full of dearth and honor.

She is his wife. That is a fact. But the truth is, Charles and I will always share something special, something that a piece of legal paper cannot undo. Even when it concerns the future emperor of California real estate.

I don't think of him as an emperor. I think of him as my king.

"I know what's going on between you and Charles, and I just want you to know that."

Diana's voice is even and calm, a windless sail across the harbor. So she does have a voice, even though she also has the prince.

The room shrinks somehow, as if all the air has been sucked out by an invisible vacuum. The mahogany bookcases, lined with the best of Whitman and Dickenson, hover over us. Kings Road has some of the most beautiful homes in all of Newport. It overlooks Mariners Mile, the section of PCH will the Ferrari dealership. Andrew is close with the owner. And the harbor. The Bay Club is in view, too. This is one of the best outlooks in all the city, in my opinion. It's also one of the streets where each home maintains its individuality, its identity. There are Tuscan homes, next to Frank Lloyd Wright homes, next to bungalows. Coexistence.

"You've got everything you ever wanted." I speak not in envy, but in realism. "You've got all the men in the world falling in love with you, and you've got two beautiful children. What more do you want?"

She could say the same of me, I guess. But we're not talking about me, are we?

We're talking about the woman who stole the hearts and minds of Newport society, a lofty bunch dripping in dollars and dalliances worth less than a pretty penny. She's young and restless, like a soap opera. She has a big heart. Maybe too big. The skin is the human body's biggest organ, and hers needs to be thicker.

As Diana stands before me, dripping in elegance and jewels once mined in the Himalayas, her eyes twinkle. I've never seen them like this, gemlike in their radiance, capturing light as a prism does.

She has poise, here, in this room. I haven't seen this before either. Maybe it's because it's just her and I. She wasn't like this at lunch, though. Then, her body language begged me for acceptance, for approval. Today, none of that is present. Today, her tiny ballerina body contracts in tight form, as during a performance of Swan Lake; both delicate and strong. Her strength is new to me. Who knew?

Chapter 52

Diana

2015

"I want my husband."

As I speak the words aloud, I wonder if they're true.

Yes, I *want* my husband, in the sense that we share a marital union. I should think that anyone in this type of relationship should want the person they're in it with.

I desire him, too, in all his moppish glory. I remember clearly the first time I saw him after Mountbatten died. I'd never seen a face so morose, so melancholy, so empty. It captured my heart. I never considered that what I felt could be pity instead of love.

Camilla stares at me. She doesn't look me in the eye. If she does, it's a flicker of acknowledgement swatted away by fear.

She should be afraid. Not in a threatening, murder mystery kind of way; I'm not a criminal. I could never harm this woman, though she's caused me great pain.

She should be afraid of losing.

"I'm sorry I'm in the way . . . and it must be hell for both of you." I empathize with their situation. I do. While it angers me to my bitter core, this ongoing tryst of theirs, I also understand their own difficulty: sharing an intimate relationship that's all but forbidden by both the family and the Firm. I don't agree with it, their commitment to carrying on. But these feelings—empathy, shame, fear, hatred—coexist within me.

"But I do know what's going on." This is the first time I've admitted it aloud, in the presence of Camilla. It feels different than it does when I accuse Charles of adultery. I wonder why that is?

Perhaps it's because, on some level, I want her approval. Whereas with Charles, I just want to be loved.

"Don't treat me like an idiot."

I'm not an idiot. Maybe I have acted like one for the duration of our courtship. I saw what I wanted to see: a princely man who showed me attention and placed me in a (seeming) position of power in his life. Wouldn't we all just like to think that we have some control over our lives? Control is an illusion.

Camilla knows this. After all, she loves a man in the shadows of all she knows she can and will never be. At least, for as long as Charles chooses rules over relationships.

That could change. Everything changes.
Just ask me.

Chapter 53

Charles

2015

I have always chosen Camilla, in every sense that I have the power to do so. Even so, that power is limited by the system in which my life exists. It's not fair. But what part of life is fair?

Especially for me. I know, *woah is me*. I want for nothing materially. What I lack is connection to emotion. Camilla shows me that and helps me. She doesn't realize it, but just existing in comfort gives me strength. She teaches my body what it feels to be safe, to be loved.

Diana is a good woman. She's just not good for me.

How could I tell my family that? How would I tell the Firm that? Better to avoid than confront the issue.

"You're an avoidant," Camilla declares as we leave her sister's birthday party. Diana has stormed home already. I'll have words for her later.

"Excuse me?"

She takes my hand. We're standing outside the Kings Road home that sits atop one of the cliffs above the bay and PCH. It's one of the best places to view the city lights; what few we have, anyway. Basically Newport Center and Fashion Island.

"You avoid situations that make you uncomfortable. You literally walk away. I've seen it. You've done it to me a million times."

"Doesn't everyone?" I'm as serious as a heart attack.

She laughs, as only she does, with inoffensive gusto. "No, honey, they don't. At least not the people that are comfortable with who they are."

I take it back. I'm offended. "Are you saying I'm insecure?"

"I'm saying," she moves in closer, so that her chin touches the top of my chest, "there's opportunity for improvement."

Before I can interrupt her, she continues, delicately and without condescension: "Let go, Charles. Instead of avoiding your feelings, feel them. Let the pain flow through you. It'll hurt, but you're strong. And it will end. Everything is temporary."

"I don't know how." I start to cry. Camilla says crying is a release—like laughing, or dancing. I wish society shared this position. Isn't it odd that we've normalized anger for men as a form of emotional expression, but crying is considered feminine, a sign of weakness? Society is consistently inconsistent.

"Sometimes you will be powerless. Let yourself feel it." She wraps her arms around me. Her petite frame barely supports me, but she's here.

"I won't abandon you."

We stand for a while in solace. We're alone, save for the starry night obscured by the glow of the office buildings in the distance.

"I'm scared."

"Me too." She kisses my cheek before we get into the car. "Control is an illusion. Let go."

And so I do.

Chapter 54

Camilla

2016

It's not about managing your emotions. It's about managing your reaction to your emotions.

I didn't always know this. Life, in all its pain and pleasure, taught me.

Andrew, that mess of a man. We were happy until we weren't. The truth is, we could never be happy. We were rich in all the ways that don't matter.

Pain and pleasure coexist in our hearts and minds. We're told to focus on the positive, the good, the glory. Forget the pain, the hurt, the grief. That can't serve you.

Ignoring it, though—that's suppression. That's avoidance. What happens when we suppress and avoid feelings? They percolate, like bubbles in champagne.

We know how much I love champagne. Sometimes the most amazing things can come from the most terrible lie.

"I'm feeling how hard this is for you in every part of my body." Sometimes empathy is the most you can do for someone.

There was a time when I used to save people. Or try to, at least. I know now that that's not possible. People need to want to save themselves. Like when an airplane pilot issues a mayday, and you're instructed to first put on your own oxygen mask before helping others. You need to save yourself before you can save another.

Healing, like most things, I realize, occurs on a spectrum. Healing and suffering are two poles of pain. Hurt, trauma, and conditioning exist in our minds. The goal is to keep our bodies safe in the present. To reconcile the two is the journey of healing.

I have my own problems. They are as apparent to me as the craters that color the moon. I'm learning to manage my reactions to my emotions, instead of managing my emotions. It's a much more achievable endeavor. Regulating emotions is like regulating the stock market; volatile, unpredictable, and pretty much a lost cause, depending on who you ask.

I feel deeply. There's no shame in that. It took me a while to learn.

I'm no saint. Some might call me a homewrecker.

But the truth is, we're all guilty of breaking some kind of rule—rules that were created by people before us who decided that, based on some kind of reaction to some kind of situation, there needed to be some structure to how things were done, to how we "do life." Rules become norms, the way we live in society. Norms become expectations. How do norms change? Over time. Change only happens when people challenge the rules, when people challenge the collective imagination of the society that made the rules.

Society is a fiction, just like money. Yet we give these things so much power. For what? For order. For peace.

I play by the rules, even when I break them. I'm not brave enough to challenge them.

Diana is. If anyone should incite change, I don't doubt it could be her. I would never admit that to her, or to Charles. I know better.

Chapter 55

Diana

2013

Morton is the one; I'm sure of it. He gets me. I can tell.

I know it while sitting across from him at Alta, the local coffee shop steps away from one of Charles' newest acquisitions. He's kind, not like most journalists. He makes you feel safe, like your story is worth telling. Maybe it's the wrinkles under his eyes, battle scars from long nights writing, researching, and thinking. Journalists must think a lot. Or maybe not at all. I'd like to think the good ones do.

Whatever the case, I feel devilish, plotting a heist in broad daylight.

Unsuspecting. Unapologetic. Undeterred.

"You must be in so much pain." His tone bestows an empathy I haven't felt from anyone. He probably sees this sort of thing all the time: the neglected wife, the oblivious husband, the other woman. A love triangle made up of deeply flawed people trying to escape their prison governed by rules and relationships.

"I am. We all are. My interest is in sharing my pain and telling my story in my own words. Can you do that?"

"I can. And I will."

He sips his spiced chai latte with poise as he presses the "record" button on his phone.

"Tell me, Diana, when did it begin?"

"Which part?"

"Your suicidal thoughts."

There's no turning back now.

They enabled me, distracted me, and eventually, abandoned me.

Chapter 56
Charles
2019

These weeds are a nightmare. And the aphids; these little bastards chew up my roses like an untrained dog chews furniture.

She's worse. Who ever thought it would get to this point of sheer loathing?

My garden gives me peace. It's green, and quiet, and all my own. No one comes here. Not because they can't, but because they don't understand. There are over a hundred varieties of roses, succulents, philodendrons, and rubber plants. There's a patch of gardenias that are hard to grow, but I still try. They smell so good. It's not a perfect place, but it's peaceful. Sometimes, it's better to choose peace over perfection.

"It's hard for everyone." Camilla knows just how to add a perspective that seems unique to the bird's eye or people who hang the moon. She's delicate as we chat over the phone—me in my office, and her in hers, mere miles apart but entirely separate hearts.

Many say I'm feminine. I know that.

Many say I'm a pathetic excuse for a leader. I know that, too.

I lack charisma, charm, all the things that make an able and revered leader.

I have a heart. Most don't think so; they see what they want to see. Their allegiance is to Diana. Who could blame them? My heart belongs to a woman who is not my wife. Per our societal norms, that is unforgivable. What about marrying someone just because they come from a stable, wealthy upbringing? What about that?

Our accountabilities are entirely unequal. That is America. That is human. That is life. I may be privileged, but I'm not dumb. How does one person affect the system into which he is born?

He doesn't. At least, not immediately. That's a generational job. A lifetime is really not that long in the grand scheme of things. My sons will have their chance to say their peace. Or piece? Both are applicable, I think.

Their lives will be so different from mine. I will model hope. I will model happiness. I will model success. My sons will have every opportunity to know what love means.

I wonder how history will remember me. (Not all the time; I'm not that vain.)

All I ever wanted was to be free. It sounds funny as I think about it. This is America—of course we are free. It's written in the stars and stripes. Yet I crave a life where I owe nothing to nobody but myself. Is that America?

Chapter 57
Camilla
2019

They are two inert gases: together, they are poisonous. Sometimes, this life is nothing but expensive misery. But someone has to do it. This fame, this level of it, feels like a form of abuse. She's a rock band on an indie label that wants her to play folk music. He's a soloist in a choir for Rock Harbor that's televised internationally. Two different harmonies with completely different expectations.

I'm not surprised by the contents of the article.

DIANA DRIVEN TO FIVE SUICIDE BIDS BY 'UNCARING' CHARLES.
I felt so desperate. I was crying my eyes out.
He said I was crying wolf. I'm not going to listen. You're always doing this to me. I'm going sailing now.
So I threw myself down the stairs. Mum comes out, absolutely horrified, shaking—she was so scared.

When I go into the Residence for a yacht party or summit meeting dinner I am a very different person. I conform to what's expected of me. They can't find fault with me when I'm in their presence. I do as I'm expected. What they say behind my back is none of my business, but I come back here and I know when I turn my light off at night I did my best.

Isn't that what you're supposed to do?

Charles is probably having an aneurysm. I need to call him.

Chapter 58

Diana

2019

He's seen it. I know he has. His phone is probably blowing up with at least twenty calls from Camilla. When I walk into the kitchen, I sit across from him like normal. The truth is, normal was lost a long time ago.

Without a word, I drop my letter in front of him on the table, next to his plate of half-eaten fruit.

I wait.

Charles,
This isn't a love letter. But know it was written from a place of love.
I'm confused. From what I've seen lately, you're confused too. It's gradually become apparent to me there is more to it. Just a general, all-inclusive "more." This is what I see:

I see you hiding from yourself, in the middle of a crisis of sorts, oscillating between security and uncertainty. You're afraid of choice, and making the wrong ones. You've already made a few wrong ones, but that's not the point. It centers around work/future career plans, around personal relationships, mixed in with anxiety for good measure. Who wouldn't be confused? We've talked a lot about these topics in different contexts, so this is somewhat old news. But recently, it's in coming to these realizations on my own that perhaps have put things in a different perspective for me.

The contents of these realizations are not in themselves significant, as much as the role they play. As you'd agree, it's not my or anyone else's job to fix you. I can support you, but only you can help yourself. And as we know, I have my problems too, and these observations aren't meant to be a dig at you or a judgment in any way. I'm just trying to "set the stage," if you will, of what I see.

Which brings me to the purpose of my letter:

I'm at a point where I'm uncomfortable with how I'm feeling, in whatever this is, and I don't like it. "It's not you, it's me" is applicable here, though the waters are a little more murky than that.

I think the world of you. I love laughing with and at you and at myself. I love your random stories about everything and nothing. I love your assortment of California succulents. I told you I wouldn't abandon you; I still mean that. I also know only I know what's right for me. The best way for me to support myself and our children (and perhaps you) right now is to leave, so there's space to figure out what needs to be figured out, for both of us.

You deserve every happiness. I know at times you don't think you do, that you may self-sabotage and punish yourself for things maybe you shouldn't. I am hard on myself too, and I suffer from it greatly. Happiness is a choice, not a result, and I hope you choose it in spite of everything else. I am trying to do the same.

I love you (okay fine, maybe this is a love letter) but it's too hard to do what I've been doing, which in some ways is also self-sabotage. As we've fought about constantly, I don't feel like I'm important to you. I have made myself sick over time, to the point of burning my throat with acid. What's more, I don't feel like we have the marriage that I want at this point. I don't feel like I've been "met halfway" in terms of finding the balance between what works for me and what works for you. I have been patient, way more than I ever have in my entire life (if anything, please take that as a compliment). Maybe the hardest thing about all of it is, at this point, I find it difficult to trust you.

I don't mean to unload all my discontents, but why stop now? That's on me for allowing myself to tolerate and suppress those feelings. I accept responsibility for that. I should have been stronger, but alas, I am me, and that is one of my many flaws: hiding my feelings in strength. But I need that pain to go away. And I have a high pain tolerance. The scars on my thighs prove it. I'm not afraid to take responsibility for myself and own it. Given the preceding and my place in all of it, it's time for me to walk away, for both our sakes and for the boys. I hope you understand.

Diana

Chapter 59

Charles

2019

At our breakfast nook, not six feet apart in physical space, but miles away in thought, we sit.

She looks at me, finally, with those sunken eyes rimmed with red. Her head is hung like she's just been defeated. Like she's been dealt the biggest blow since Abercrombie & Fitch rebranded.

Me?

I am seething. I don't have enough breath to breathe.

"I'm sorry. I didn't see any other way."

The worst part is, I believe her.

There's nothing worse than betrayal. How could she do this? One minute, we're sitting here, living our married life over eggs benedict and our respective versions of good coffee. Mine is simple: black. Hers is some version of a Starbucks concoction that I can't pronounce. It's not the happiest, but it's real. Then, the next minute, our lives blow up in smoke like a burning pile of manure—putrid and suffocating.

"I know you may never want to speak to me again, and I know you will because of the boys. I will always care for you, even if I can't control how you feel about me. Because I can't control how you feel about me any more than I can control when the sun rises, or that it rises at all."

"She's my one true love." I didn't know what else to say but the truth. We've been through hell and high water. It's time for honesty.

"I thought we were it, the end game. I tried so hard to be what you need. It never worked. I loved you so much. It wasn't enough."

"I never loved you."

But I did. I loved her, once upon a time. And I still love her, as someone would love the mother of their children. I just don't love her in the way she wants to be loved.

At the beginning, we would laugh and cry and she would look at me like I was the only person in the world. She stroked me, my body and my ego. I guess there's a chance it wasn't love. Maybe it was anxiety. Maybe it was adrenaline. Maybe it was the peace I got from my family not bothering me anymore.

Now? It's the end.

Maybe it was all meant to be.

Diana

It's over. I'm free to leave.

Charles

It's over. I'm free to breathe.

Camilla

It's over. I'm free to love.

Thank You!

I am so appreciative of you taking the time to read my book. This novel is very personal to me, and I hope that sentiment came through in my words.

If you enjoyed *The Crown of the Sea*, and would be willing to spare just two or three minutes . . . please share your review of the book on my website:

www.bysarasalam.com

Reviews help me get the book into as many hands as possible, and support my work as an author for the long-term (my dream!).

I'm grateful for your support and look forward to sharing more of my work with you!

Acknowledgments

I got the idea for this story while listening to a podcast series about Princess Diana in late 2020. The story of three rich, deeply flawed people humanized for me the idea that the wealthy, while perhaps more comfortable, feel pain the same way everyone else does. I grew up in Newport Beach, where wealth is a way of life for many. So I thought, what if some version of these people lived in Newport today? What would that look like? Thus, *The Crown of the Sea* came to life.

It was fun to draw parallels between a family so loved and hated by history, and a lifestyle I grew up around and witnessed in both childhood and adulthood. I have no judgement, truly, for this way of life. We all have our shit. I see so much value in relatability—that while we all have different contexts for how we experience the world, we are all human. We all have physiological, mental, and emotional responses to the circumstances we find ourselves in, especially in relationships. Relationships, at least for me, are the most beautiful part of living and being alive. And yet for many of us, myself included, we weren't necessarily taught what it takes to build and grow our relationships in ways that are healthy, fulfilling, and authentic. We learn from our models, who don't necessarily get it right all the time. Nor should they; that's an unrealistic expectation. We are all flawed. It's no one's fault, but it's our responsibility to do better when we know better. There's a lot of research out there these days to help us do that, to learn the tools it takes to nurture and maintain happy, healthy relationships with the people we love. This book exposes some of the darker sides of toxic relationships—how not having the tools can perpetuate and exacerbate the issues. That is very real. I guess what I'm saying is, there's no shame in flaws; I only see opportunities for growth. Carpe diem.

As with all of my work, my goal is to entertain, educate, and empower my readers. I find value in learning new things, and I do my best to pass my own observations and learnings along to my readers. The content in this novel in particular may feel heavy at times. I wrote it during a period in my life when I had highs and lows, amidst the backdrop of a pandemic, and struggled to be hopeful. I see that in my writing. That is raw, that is real life, and that's what I feel compelled to share at this stage in my author journey.

As always, I'm grateful for the support of family and friends who motivate me to keep going. To MSG, for starting a writing club and commitment to the craft that moves us. To the royals, who get a lot of good and bad press, who like everyone else, simply do the best they can with the awareness they have. And for my hometown, where I made my memories, wrote them down, and turned them into meaningful messages to share with the world. I'm thankful every day for the opportunity to write in the place that has shaped so much of me. The poetry of it all is not lost on me.

A Note About the Author

Sara Salam is an award-winning author, editor, and poet. Published since age 11, Sara writes nonfiction, fiction, and poetry. In addition to her work as an author, Sara spent seven seasons working in professional sports: five with the Boston Red Sox (2013 World Series Champion!) and two with the LA Clippers. During this time, she primarily focused on human resources strategy, including diversity and inclusion, talent acquisition, and professional development. Sara is a proud UCLA Bruin and active in her community of Newport Beach. She enjoys writing, yoga, and the beach.

To join Sara Salam's email list for updates on her books, scan the QR code below:

© 2021 Sara Salam

www.bysarasalam.com

@bysarasalam

Sara Salam

www.ingramcontent.com/pod-product-compliance
Lightning Source LLC
LaVergne TN
LVHW040138080526
838202LV00042B/2954